THE COVENANT

By the same author

The Unholy
Blood Rite

The Covenant

MICHAEL FALCONER ANDERSON

St. Martin's Press
New York

THE COVENANT. Copyright © 1988 by Michael Falconer Anderson.
All rights reserved. Printed in the United States of America. No part
of this book may be used or reproduced in any manner whatsoever
without written permission except in the case of brief quotations
embodied in critical articles or reviews. For information, address
St. Martin's Press, 175 Fifth Avenue, New York, N.Y. 10010.

Library of Congress Cataloging-in-Publication Data

Anderson, Michael Falconer.
    The covenant / Michael Falconer Anderson.
        p.   cm.
    ISBN 0-312-02179-8
    I. Title.
PR6051.N396C68   1988
823'.914—dc19   88-14781
                                                                                                                           CIP

First published in Great Britain by Robert Hale Limited.

10 9 8 7 6 5 4 3 2

Prologue

ONE.
The word was not spoken, not transmitted, not sent forth by anyone, not carried by any messenger.

It simply came into being and woke him.

Like a muffled alarm.

Woke him from his place beyond time and space and the twelve dimensions. Here there was no flesh, no warmth, no light, no beauty, few sensations worthy of mention.

Just darkness and eons of time for him to contemplate it, to seethe with anger and plan his revenge.

And now the day had come.

The Day of the One.

One

Aragarr, Scotland

The woman was panting by the time she reached the top of the hill and looked down into the moonlight-spattered darkness of the glen beyond but she did not slow down. She hurried forward to the great stone which stood in the centre of the flat, heather-covered plateau and reached out and touched it, sighing gently, letting her eyes fall closed.

After a moment, her fingers began to search for the familiar clefts and gaps and holes which thousands of years of wind and rain and winter frost had scarred onto the face of the boulder.

They were there, unchanged.

She began to climb and reached the top easily and confidently in a few minutes.

There she undressed, oblivious to the chilly night wind which snatched at her hair, prickled across her skin, hardened her nipples.

Naked, she knelt down, her eyes closed, her hands raised to the sky, palms uplifted, and began to mutter the words of the ritual.

Once her eyes flicked open and for an instant it was as if there was another glen beyond the glen below her and another beyond that one, as if there were hundreds of glens all aligned, like a great slice in the earth. And beyond that ...

Doors beyond doors, all opening, all perfectly aligned, all synchronised by destiny.

When the ritual was finished a strange light seemed to fill her brain.

She looked down into the glen again and saw that it was just a glen now, trees and stones, hollows and rises twisted grotesquely by the moonlight.

But she knew the truth.

She dressed, smiling slightly, climbed down the stone and headed back the way she had come. At the edge of the plateau she turned and whispered a word into the night.

'Two,' she said softly.

Los Angeles

'It just doesn't feel like it ought to,' Al McBaith said, gulping another mouthful of beer and putting his feet up on the coffee table in front of him. He realised he was slurring his words.

Six hours before he had signed the last of the forms, handed in his Smith and Wesson .38 and ceased to be a member of the Los Angeles Police Department. After twenty years, three months and two days he had decided to take his forty per cent pension and accept a job as head of security with a mining company in Oregon.

He had expected some kind of sense of change, of departure, some immediate feeling that he was stepping through a door, starting out on a new venture, heading for a new frontier. But it wasn't there.

Instead he had a strange feeling of threat, of danger, an inexplicable fear. It had been there for the past month and he had tried to analyse it without coming up with any answers.

'What ... what don't feel like it ought to?' Johnny Borowski said.

McBaith didn't answer, just sat staring at nothing, thinking, his powerful face tense despite the booze he had consumed. The face was dominated by a large, broad nose and a thrusting chin with a deep cleft slightly off-centre. It was a face that looked well-travelled, lived in, as if each minute of its forty-one years had been an ordeal that had left him numb and hardened. There was grey in his short, curly brown hair and thick moustache and lines around his green eyes, long slits in the tanned, leathery skin. The eyes were set deep beneath shaggy, black eyebrows which met in the centre, and they were tired, watchful and world-weary. He was six-two with immense shoulders and proud of the fact that his scales had read 185 for the past ten years.

'What don't feel like it ought to?' Borowski said again.

McBaith explained his feelings as best he could but left out any mention of the feeling of danger.

(Why? Why didn't he tell Borowski about that? What was there about it that had to be kept a secret?)

He ended by saying: 'I just don't feel a thing. I don't feel as if anything has changed. I don't feel like I'm really moving on.'

Borowski shrugged, a drunken exaggerated shrug, new lines appearing on his face and creasing across the pink plateau of his bald head as he grimaced in an expression that said *Who knows and what does it matter anyway.*

'I guess it could take months for it to sink in, Al,' he said. 'You've been a homicide cop for a long time. Maybe you'll miss it.' He gave a brief chuckle over the last two words.

'Yeah,' McBaith said dryly. 'Just think, I might never get to see another dead body.'

Dead body.

The words stabbed through his mind like twin electric shocks and when they were gone the face hung there.

The face of the tall black man with the pencil moustache. He looked the way he had just as McBaith had squeezed the trigger, the instant before the .38 bullet had blown the side of his head away. Surprised and resigned, both at the same time. Surprised, McBaith had guessed later, because death surprises us all. Resigned because he was a loser who had known for a long time his luck was running out.

McBaith shook his head and blinked and the image of the man's face slipped back into his subconscious. His retirement celebration had started at five-thirty, taken in a dozen bars and ended at his apartment. There had been a crowd at the beginning but only ten or so had stayed the pace and returned with him to the place he called home to drink his Budweiser and Scotch. Then they had peeled off one by one (saying 'Take care of yourself, Al' and shaking his hand as they went) until now only Borowski was left.

There had been a time when he and Borowski had been close friends, visiting each other's homes with their wives and children, but both marriages had broken up now. McBaith's wife had remarried, to a doctor in Chicago, and Borowski's was living with her mother in Monterey. Three years before, Borowski had transferred to narcotics and since then they had only seen each other for a beer once in a while, maybe four times a year.

Borowski grinned: 'You know your problem?'

'No, what's that?'

'You didn't have the right kind of last day.'

'Why's that?'

'Well ... you're supposed to arrive at your desk hoping for a quiet day and then find a crazy has gone on the rampage or get a death threat from some guy you sent down years ago. It's in all the paperbacks. You're supposed to get shot at and seduced and be involved in a long car chase.'

McBaith laughed. 'Do I get killed in the end?' he said.

Borowski began to chuckle and it dissolved into a high-pitched lunatic giggle. 'You have ... to wait ... for the last page,' he yelled.

'You're nuts, you know that,' McBaith said as Borowski's laughter became a wheezing pant.

Borowski wiped laughter-tears from his eyes and said: 'So what now for Al McBaith?'

'I'm going to Europe, didn't I tell you?'

'You mentioned something about it.'

'I don't have to be in Oregon for three months. I'll spend a couple of months in Europe – Scotland mostly – then I think I'll get over to Chicago and see Tina and the kids. I might even look up a couple of my brothers. I've got six you know.'

'Yeah, you told me that once.'

'I think my old man wanted to populate the entire United States with little McBaiths.'

Borowski finished his beer, crushed the empty can in his hand and tugged the ring-pull off another.

'Why Scotland?' he said.

'What?'

'You said Scotland mostly.'

'It's where the name comes from – McBaith. My grandparents came from a little place on the coast. About six months ago I started to get this urge to go there ... '

'Back to your roots,' Borowski said.

'I guess you could put it like that. I'm an American through and through but it's like ... ' He thought a moment then said: 'It's like there's a hunk of me that's something else. I put an ad in a newspaper over there, hoping I'd get in touch with a distant relative ... '

'And did you?'

'Yeah. There's a guy called McBaith still living in the village where my grandparents came from. His grandfather was my grandfather's youngest brother. He's got some kind of little hotel and he's offered to put me up for as long as I want. We've been writing to each other and I've found out all kinds of things. The house my grandfather was born in is still there ... it's a ruin now, the roof's caved in, but I'll be able to see it.'

'I hope you have a great time.'

'Sure.'

McBaith locked his hands behind his head and tried to blink away sudden tiredness.

Borowski sipped at his beer without speaking for a moment then said: 'Do you remember Freddie Antilla?' That started the reminiscences that went on for hours.

It was almost dawn when McBaith called a cab for Borowski.

'Give me a call when you're in L.A. again,' Borowski said at the door.

'I will.'

'Have fun in Europe.'
'I'll do that.'
'And drop me a postcard from this famous place where the McBaiths come from. What's it called anyway?'
'Aragarr,' McBaith said.

As the cab drove away, the word hung in his mind.

Aragarr.

He closed the door slowly and found the sense of danger and fear rising through him, intensifying beyond anything he had ever felt before.

Why?

He tried to analyse it as he undressed.

It wasn't like the gut-wrenching fear when a sniper's bullet had ploughed through the roof of his car one hot afternoon just after he had given evidence that had sent a Colombian drug pedlar away for a long time; not the same as the nerve-jangling apprehension when he had tried to talk a kid with a shotgun into coming out of the liquor store he had robbed; not like the time a Puerto Rican pimp had pulled a knife on him and made a stab for his face. Not like any of those. It was like a first-cousin to fear, a memory of what childhood terrors were like, a ghostly stiletto sliding between his shoulder-blades, as chilly and insubstantial as early-morning sea mist. He grunted, angry and irritated, as he got into bed. Odd feelings didn't scare men like Al McBaith. It just didn't happen. A bullet in the stomach, a car accident that left him paralysed, being kicked so badly he ended up with brain damage – those things would have scared him if he had let himself think about them. Even Aids, cancer, leprosy and a hundred other things.

But not odd feelings.

The image of the black man with the pencil moustache he had shot dead slipped into his conscious mind again.

Had to be something to do with that.

Guilt. That was it.

He hadn't been the first man McBaith had ever shot but he had been the first he had ever killed.

The crazy son-of-a-bitch had been trying to rob a

garage ...
   With a replica pistol for Christ sake.
   And he had pointed it at McBaith even after he had said, 'Police, hold it right there ... '
   Not that.
   The words came to him suddenly, abruptly closing the file on the black man in his brain.
   It *wasn't* the black man who was causing all this.
   So what could it be?
   Maybe he needed an analyst? Maybe he felt guilty about Tina and the kids, maybe he was sliding into menopause, maybe he had hit that time of life when he was too aware of his own mortality.
   Aragarr.
   The word tumbled back into his mind as he descended towards sleep.
   All this had nothing to do with his life or the past, something told him.
   The fear was coming from the future.
   From Aragarr.
   And it had been there ever since he had made the decision to go to Scotland.

Aragarr, Scotland

Secluded chalet. That was what the advertisement had said and that was what the Youngers got.
   It stood near the top of one of the hills overlooking Aragarr, just beyond the treeline, where the face of the hill became rocky, pitted with boulders, scarred by jagged outcrops of stone; where nothing grew but the hardiest grass and heather.
   Driving up in the fading sunlight Graham Younger had thought the hill looked like the head of a bald man. The pine forest represented the hair at the back and sides and the desolate, bare top resembled a bald dome.
   'Just perfect,' Moira Younger had said hardly above a

whisper as their car climbed the steep, rutted track through the forest. It seemed the ideal place to get away from it all – neighbours, work, friends, cars, city noise, daily commuting, the children (who were equally happy to wave goodbye to their parents for a week and spend the time with doting grandparents).

She wanted to soak up silence, slow down the pace of her life for a while, read some good books, listen to her Grieg and Mendelssohn tapes, watch the sun set over Loch Aragarr and be totally alone with her husband for the first time in three years. *Bliss.*

She was delighted when she saw the chalet. It had a large lounge on the ground floor with French windows which opened onto a verandah that ran the full length of the chalet and provided a wonderful view down across the still, silent sea of pines to Aragarr to the north and Loch Aragarr to the south. It was clean and comfortable, tastefully decorated and had a shower, bath, sauna and colour television just as the brochure had promised. The bedroom was reached via a steep wooden stairway in the centre of the lounge.

When she had finished searching the place for a flaw with her typical pessimism (and found none) she had said again 'Just perfect.'

After they had eaten, he had rubbed his hands together as he always did when he was contented and announced: 'Right, I'm going to have a shower and take a walk down to the village for a beer. How about you?'

'I'll finish the unpacking.'

'But you're on holiday,' he said, appealing to her.

'The bags still have to be unpacked. You go ahead, but take the car.'

'The car, why?'

'It's dark out there now. You have to go through the forest.'

'It's not much more than a quarter of a mile to the main road,' he said, 'and about the same from there to Aragarr.'

'But ... '

'I'd rather not drive up that track at night. There were

some pretty bad bumps and holes. I might lose the exhaust. Besides, what do you think is out there ... wolves?'

'I wouldn't walk through there alone at night for anything,' she said.

'It's a Scottish pine forest for goodness' sake, not the Brazilian jungle. There are no anacondas, no man-eating plants. I didn't come all the way up here to tear around in a car all the time. I want to walk and get the feel of the place. Life at a slower pace, that was the idea, remember?'

She nodded reluctantly.

'See if you can see the shop when you're down there,' she said as he disappeared up the stairs, stripping off his jumper.

'OK.'

'The travel agent said there was a store where we could get anything we needed. I'll do all the shopping tomorrow.'

'It shouldn't be hard to find,' he laughed. 'Aragarr is not exactly Princes Street, Edinburgh.' She slipped on a coat as protection against the night chill and stepped out onto the verandah. There was a full moon and the bay far below her was bathed in a yellow pall. The lights of Aragarr twinkled away to her left like a cluster of fireflies in a crook of the bay where the gentle sweep of the beach met a thrusting, rocky promontory that Moira thought looked like the back of a giant lizard which had gone down to catch a fish.

She went inside when her husband came downstairs, clean-shaven and refreshed after his shower. He was wearing a roll-neck pullover, jeans and running shoes.

'Better wear a coat,' she said.

'It's not that cold. I'll be fine. It's not the Antarctic you know, and it isn't even winter yet.'

'All right. If you want to play the intrepid adventurer ... but don't blame me if you get a chill.'

'I won't,' he promised. 'I'll be back in half an hour,' he added, kissing her briefly, his dutiful going-to-work or going-to-the-pub kiss.

She stood at the French windows watching him strolling through the moonlight and waved as he raised his right hand and disappeared into the forest.

Younger was surprised at how dark it was among the trees and had no sooner thought *Thank God for the moon* than he saw a dark cloud begin to drift across one corner of it, dimming the weak yellow light that illuminated the track. It occurred to him that if the moonlight was shut out altogether he might be in total blackness.

Go back to the chalet, said a voice in his head and a brief laugh escaped from his lips. He hadn't gone fifty yards and already he was thinking he had made a mistake. *Go back and get the car.*

He shook his head slowly, knowing what Moira would say. He could hear her words already. *No wolves eh? No anacondas, no man-eating plants. Nothing to be afraid of.* She would have her little joke — and what could he say in reply?

Anyway, it wasn't that he was scared exactly. It was just that ... when he went for a walk he was used to cars and street lights and people and *noise*.

Noise.

He listened. There was no sound at all. Was that normal? Weren't there always noises of some kind in a forest?

He reached the first bend, aware that half of the moon had disappeared now, the dark cloud edging across it, nibbling away at it inch by inch.

Here the track was like a ravine cut through a solid mass; it was bordered by tall trees wrapped in ghostly yellow light and beyond them there was only blackness — no shapes, no movement, just what looked like an impenetrable black wall.

Apprehension began to stir within him, sending a rash of tiny pinprick sensations up the back of his neck.

Go back, a voice in his head told him. It was like someone whispering in his ear and it startled him. What excuse could he use if he did return to the chalet? Could he say he had forgotten something? Could he ...

This was stupid. It was not as if he was scared. What was there for a thirty-seven-year-old accountant to be afraid of? He was no child who could be easily spooked by darkness.

There was nothing out there but trees and brush. No bogeyman. No things that go bump in the night. No wolves. No anacondas. No spirits of lost souls wandering in the night.
Spirits of lost souls.
Jesus in heaven, what had made him think of such a thing?
He stopped dead.
Go back and get the car. It was a silly idea to walk. Getting the car was the sensible thing to do. Moira had been right; why didn't he admit it?
But again he thought of what she might say. There was no doubt she would throw his words back at him. *This is not the Brazilian jungle you know. Intrepid adventurer eh?*
'Stoppit,' he rasped, irritated at himself, and started down the track again. 'Stoppit and don't be so damned stupid.'
He would be on the main road in five minutes and in the pub in another ten.
He walked on at a brisk pace and entered a clearing just as the pale light faded dramatically. Looking up at the moon, he saw that almost all of it was hidden now, just a tiny piece was visible, like a thin slice of melon. He blinked, stared, tried to will the cloud away, but it rolled remorselessly on.
That was when he heard something rushing through the forest, heading straight for him. Moving fast.
His mind ran wild with possibilities. A stag? Some bird of prey caught in the high branches? *A mad dog?*
Then he saw it, a reddish-brown blur about a foot long scampering across the carpet of pine needles.
A wildcat? A weasel? A ...
It skittered to a halt in a patch of heather in the clearing, about ten feet from where he stood.
A stoat.
It watched him for a moment, crouched, tensed, its tiny sharp teeth bared, its weasel face quivering, then rose onto its back legs and began to do a strange dance, jumping and twisting, its white belly seeming to glow in the weak

moonlight, its black tail flicking about. It started to squeak in explosive little yelps then shot towards him aggressively.

He took two quick steps backwards. *Stoats didn't attack people.*

Did they?

They lived by hunting small game and were in turn hunted by man for their fur (Ermine? The fur was called ermine, wasn't it?)

He stamped his foot.

'Go away.'

It came to within three feet of him then danced away, still on its hind legs.

His heart was beating wildly now and there was a drumming in his temples. Being afraid annoyed him (how could he be scared of such a little thing?) and he stepped forward and aimed a kick at it. It scampered back, crouched low, gave a final shriek and was gone, darting over the pine needles into the blackness of the forest.

He shifted his gaze back to the moon again and saw that all that was left now was a tiny triangle in the top right-hand corner. The cloud drifted on, the triangle shrank, the light weakened.

Then the moon was gone altogether and all the light in the clearing went with it. He was in total darkness, as if he was standing in a pit.

Of course the cloud would move on soon, he told himself. But was there any need to wait? His eyes would become accustomed to the dark.

He paused a moment, standing in the centre of the clearing then walked straight ahead, his eyes picking out vague shapes where there were tree trunks and branches.

He walked fifteen paces like a blind man then his hand encountered a tree and he drew it back surprised. He told himself he must have swung to the left, away from the spot where the track left the clearing, and moved back to his right. Then his right hand brushed a tree and he felt his feet sinking into pine needles.

He had wandered away from the track, away from the

clearing. He was in the trees. *Stay where you are. Don't go any further from the track. Just wait.*

He calmed his panic by telling himself there was a funny side to all this. At least it would be funny to other people. He would be a laughing stock if he got lost on a walk to the pub. My God, what if they had to call out the rescue teams. He's never live that down. Moira would be calling him the intrepid adventurer and Jungle Jim for years. He began to laugh but there was a nervous thread through it, more than a touch of hysteria.

Just how funny was this situation, he wondered. Was he in danger? It was a cold night. If he didn't make it back to the chalet, was he facing hypothermia? What could there be out there in the darkness? Stags? Adders? He peered at the ground around his feet, searching for snakes, but found nothing but pine needles.

Then a glow away to his right made him snatch his head up. It was the track, about twenty feet away. The moon had reappeared and was illuminating the track again but none of the light was penetrating the tight ranks of trees around him.

It was as he stamped his way back through the pine needles (it was like walking on cushions, he thought) that he saw the stoat again. Doing its little dance in the middle of the clearing.

What did it want?

What could ...

Then he saw the second stoat. It was doing the same dance, chittering and yelping at him. He ducked, pushed his way through the low branches and stepped into the clearing.

Not two stoats.

Five now.

And another ...

Over there to his right, snaking into the clearing, rearing up onto its hind legs and joining the dance.

He was definitely going back to the chalet.

'Get away ... go on,' he shouted, stamping his feet.

He marched back across the clearing, heading for the point where the track climbed back to the chalet.
Not six stoats now.
Twenty at least.
The clearing was filled with a yelping din.
It was as he turned up the track that something nameless and very cold settled in beside his heart.
The track was covered in stoats (*Thirty. No, fifty. More*), all dancing, their white bellies seeming to shine against the dimness of the night.
'Get away.' His voice, breaking.
They didn't move, didn't scatter. They held their ground.
He was cut off.
He turned back into the clearing and froze.
It was filled with stoats.
A hundred.
No. Two hundred.
Dancing, chittering, shrieking.
Watching him.
What could they want?
Should he run?
Get a big stick?
Should he ...
Then the light began to fade again.
He jerked his head up.
A cloud, moving fast, was sweeping across the face of the moon.
Not that. Oh no. Not that.
He bit his lip, realised his knees were shaking, and began to run, heading downhill again.
Stoats just didn't do this, did they?
They didn't gather and dance ...
He left the clearing just as the light in the track disappeared as if it had been sucked away. He was running in a tunnel now. No vision. Only sound. He hit a tree running at full speed, spun away and ran on, feeling blood trickling down his face.

But the chittering wasn't diminishing.

It was all around him now, and there were other sounds. Hundreds of tiny feet darting along the track, scampering through pine needles.

A small body hit his leg, bounced away.

Then something hit his thigh. This time he felt a sharp pain as it was knocked away.

And blood. On his leg.

An invisible shape snapped at the back of his calf and held, tiny teeth biting through his jeans, ripping at his flesh. He swung a fist down and punched the furry form but it held on.

In his mind there was a strange, crazy jabbering now and it seemed to keep time with the chittering of the stoats.

Another jumped at his thigh and held. Teeth snatched at his shirt, his fingers, his running shoes, his face.

He flailed his arms about uselessly but couldn't knock them away. His body was a hundred shafts of burning pain now.

And his legs were buckling.

He didn't know how many were on him, snapping and shrieking, but their weight and his terror made him slip and fall to one knee. He continued to try to knock them away but realised they were all over him.

Panic.

Searing fear ...

Then calm.

He was numb when he felt himself folding slowly to the ground, toppling over in stages.

Countless sharp-toothed mouths bit and tore at him but now it felt as if they were biting some heavy overcoat he was wearing. There was no pain. As he felt himself drifting away, he was only vaguely aware that they were still actually biting his flesh.

Eating him.

Intent on killing him.

Moira Younger was in the shower when she heard the

sound of glass smashing. She stopped singing immediately, the words catching in her throat.

'Graham. Graham, is that you?'

No answer.

Not Graham.

She ran a towel briefly across her body then wrapped it around herself and dripped her way across the bedroom. Reaching the stairway that descended into the lounge, she hurried down, eager to find out what was happening before fear set in, before her imagination started playing tricks on her.

'Graham!'

It had to be Graham.

She was halfway down the stairs when she felt a sudden chill, a sharp draught. Then she saw the huge jagged hole in the French window. Through the opening she could see the distant rocky promontory jutting out from the beach far below, a large expanse of night sky and a full moon.

How on earth ...

A branch? The wind?

But they weren't that close to any trees. And there was no gale blowing.

The window must have been flawed, cracked before they arrived.

Damn. She'd have to call the emergency number the travel agent had given her and ...

Then something caught her eye.

A brown shape leaping across a two-feet space between the settee and the drinks cabinet.

A rat?

She shivered with revulsion.

Why would a rat jump through the window?

She tiptoed down the stairs then rushed for the cupboard near the front door where she had seen a broom.

Whatever the creature was, it was about to be shooed out the front door.

She grabbed the broom and spun around just as the stoat reappeared, watching her now, chittering, standing on its hind legs. The fur on its stomach was a gorgeous white, she thought through her sudden fright.

'Get,' she shouted, reaching for the front door.

But her hand never found the handle, never opened the door. It froze in mid-air as she heard the drumming of tiny feet on the verandah outside.

And saw the stoats begin to surge in through the broken window.

Hundreds of them.

The woman stood in a pool of moonlight in the centre of the clearing for a long time, not moving, her face impassive, her eyes staring into the blackness of the pine forest. No sound came from the trees, no breathing of the wind or scurrying of animals.

As the moon slipped behind a cloud, leaving her in total darkness, she blinked and a smile tugged at the ends of her mouth.

'Three,' she said and the word seemed to whisper away through the trees like a tiny night-bird.

Two

The moonlight reflected in the youth's shining eyes made them look as if they were glowing.

Ally Taggart was standing alone on the beach half a mile from Aragarr, staring at the small waves which rose to dim hump-backed outlines then tumbled over and over in a mass of white water which gurgled to within inches of his feet then withdrew with a hissing, sucking sound.

The waves were breaking so *slowly*.

He had never noticed that before.

Why had that fact always escaped him?

They rose ...

... and seemed to hang there for a long time before folding forward as slowly as oozing mud.

Then the white water appeared.

But it was not really water at all.

It was millions of diamonds, each with a character of its own. If he stared intently at one spot he could pick out a single diamond and see it glittering and shining, more beautiful than anything he had ever seen before.

And when he did that sometimes he saw things in that single diamond and it spoke to him in a low voice, telling him what he had to do.

Sometimes he saw colours that he had never seen before, colours that did not belong on the earth, and sometimes he saw the faces of beckoning women. But most often he saw something indescribable – it was like a shining, warm eternity of exquisite, unimaginable beauty where peace and excitement were combined in endless ecstasy.

He knew he could have that whenever he wanted it – all he had to do was fly. And he could fly. He could take off from a high cliff or the top branches of a pine and soar forever if he wanted to. Why had he never known that before? Why were people all so blind?

He knelt down in the damp sand on a sudden impulse and thrust his hand into the gurgling water. A tiny white bubble – *no*, a diamond – stuck to his finger.

He thrilled at the chill of its tiny form on his knuckles and held it up to his ear (he knew that was what he was meant to do this time). It whispered a single word to him – a name.

Ferguson.

He had known it was going to say that. He knew what he had to do. The diamonds had told him before.

He had to kill Mr Ferguson because Mr Ferguson had done something really bad.

He stood up and held his hand close up to his face, watching the diamond slowly dissolve, feeling its coolness running between the hairs on the back of his hand.

When it was gone, he turned and started back along the beach towards Aragarr, his head hunched down into his black polo-neck pullover in a bid to protect his face from the cold wind that whipped along the sand.

A combination of a sudden grumbling as the jetliner hit a spot of turbulence and a nudge on the elbow snatched McBaith out of his daydream.

He looked around at the chubby, red-faced man in the next seat and the man said, 'Headin' for London?' in a Southern accent.

'Yeah,' McBaith said with no friendliness in his tone. 'A couple of days in London then on to Scotland.'

'Scotland. Fine country Scotland. I was up there once, in the far north. I went for a long walk out of this little town and, I'll tell you, when you get out of sight of civilisation it's like ... like history, you could be living a million years ago. You could be in the Stone Age or something. There's nothing that tells you you're living in the twentieth century. I walked a long time and just when I thought maybe I was lost ... ' He paused and chuckled. ' ... I turned a corner and there was a bar and two boys from Atlanta – oilmen they were – sitting on a wall drinking Southern Comfort. It's a funny world ... small world too.'

McBaith nodded jerkily, trying to keep an expression of irritation from his face. He didn't feel like talking and the daydream the man had interrupted had been poignant and personal.

He had been staring down at the Atlantic far below and the thought had occurred to him that his grandparents had crossed that same ocean seventy-six years before, going the other way.

How different had their journeys been, he had wondered. It couldn't have been much fun for a fisherman and his wife travelling steerage and as near as dammit to flat broke. No pleasant plane journey for them, with a comfortable seat and drinks and meals brought along at the touch of a button.

McBaith had never known his grandmother – she had died just after his father had been born. But he remembered his grandfather. He had been a tall man with white hair and a long white beard and McBaith had recalled that when he had sat on his grandfather's knee the old man had been very warm. He remembered that the old man had spoken in a lilting way that sounded like he was singing and that he spoke another language too, which he called 'the Gaelic'.

McBaith recollected that he had once said to his grandfather, 'Is that a Scottish accent?' and his grandfather had laughed and answered, 'No, it's an American accent, Alexander. If you had heard my accent when I lived in Scotland you'd never have understood me.'

He remembered the old man telling him about Scotland where there were great mountains capped with snow and where a few men owned all the land and never gave the rest of the people any chance to get any of it and the sea teemed with fish ('There were so many fish, Alexander, that when I was a boy I used to just stand by the sea with a jar and whistle and before you could say Bonnie Prince Charlie a fish would jump into my jar.')

Then he had remembered the day when his grandfather had been supposed to come and see him, but hadn't. When he had asked why, his father had looked grim and told him to go and play. He had pieced together the terrible truth from occasional words and snatches of conversation he had overheard as his parents talked in another room.

His grandfather had gone away, to another place, for good.

A place called *being dead*.

And he wasn't coming back. Not ever.

'You a tourist?' the red-faced man was saying now.

'Kind of,' McBaith said stiffly. 'I'll be looking up relatives.'

The man introduced himself as Bobby Low, a businessman from Memphis.

'First time over ... in the old country?'

'Yeah.'

McBaith felt his irritation growing, his face tightening. He blamed Low for the loss of the daydream and telling himself that the man was only trying to be friendly didn't help.

'I get over every once in a while,' Low said, 'to do a little business, you know. I buy and sell. Old stuff, antiques, paintings. It's hard to get them out of the country sometimes but I ... ' He waved his hand through the air in a gesture that suggested he was intimating shady practices and lowered his voice theatrically. 'Me and my partners have our methods, know what I mean?'

'Yeah, I get the message.'

'What do you do?'

McBaith considered saying he was in the security business, or even in plastics or insurance, but decided this was too good an opportunity to end the conversation and go in search of his daydream and the memories of his grandfather.

'I'm a cop,' he said.

A little of the redness in Low's face drained away.

'Jesus.' He tried to laugh but it came out as a nervous triple-hiss and there was no mirth in his eyes. 'You're off-duty, I hope. I mean ... I was only kiddin' ... about ... you know, what I said.'

McBaith turned the emotional knife. 'I'm on special assignment for Scotland Yard,' he said and looked out the window again as Low grinned awkwardly and buried his face in a magazine.

But there was no pleasant daydream there now, no poignant memories. Instead he found a strange sensation washing over him, a feeling he couldn't describe.

It grew stronger and stronger and reached a peak as he disembarked at Gatwick.

He tried to analyse it and the words *déjà-vu* came into his mind.

Why?

He had never been to Britain before.

His brow was furrowed with concentration as he strolled through the passenger terminal.

No, not déjà-vu. It wasn't quite as if it had all happened before. It was as if something was telling him that what was happening was destiny, meant to be; as if he'd had a sudden premonition that his journey had never quite been in his hands, under his control. That something had borne him along.

He felt as if he was ...

Going home.

Going to a place he had once known.

Dammit he had never been in Aragarr before.

But the feeling persisted, that he knew the place, was familiar with it, was going to a place which was not alien to him, but welcoming and known.

Going home.

Brian Ferguson was angry, but no angrier than he usually was. He was one of those men who was always indignant about something, complaining about some minute failing in the world around him, bitter about life, ready to be offended by an imagined slight. He lived in a state of constant irritation. If he wasn't resentful about something that was going wrong on his farm – and there was *always* some little thing – then he was fuming about his wife or his lack of cash or tourists who pitched tents on his land.

Muriel had left the year before, after ten years of marriage. She hadn't even told him face-to-face that she was going, just taken Moreen, their little girl, and left him a note. *A note, for Christ sake.* After ten years all she could do was write a note. And not much of a note either. 'Brian,' it had said (and the words were burned on his brain now). 'It's no good us going on. I can't stand it anymore and it's not fair on Moreen. I won't be coming back. Muriel.'

What wasn't fair on Moreen? That was what he could never work out. Hadn't he clothed and fed them? Hadn't he given them everything they could want? *Good riddance.* That was the best way to look at it, he decided. They'd had everything he could give them and that hadn't been enough. Well, just let them come crawling back one day and then they'd see what he'd say. He wasn't going to give anyone a second chance. *A second chance?* No fear of that.

He liked to imagine himself ordering Muriel out if she ever showed her face at the farm again. Someone had once told him at the Jacobite Arms in Aragarr that he was lucky Muriel hadn't sued him for money to help with Moreen's upbringing. *Lucky.* She'd had ten years of his money and she wouldn't get another penny.

He was driving his harvester west along a one-lane road that descended towards Aragarr, his headlights creating a funnel of light between the stone walls which bordered the road, when he saw the car coming towards him.

The car slowed, but Ferguson didn't. He carried on at the same speed, both edges of the harvester swishing through the weeds at the roadside, the vehicle's width ruling out any possibility of the car getting past.

The harvester drew level with a spot where the road widened and there was a gate into a field. Ferguson could have pulled into the side but he didn't. He bit his lower lip, relishing the situation. He didn't recognise the car – it was big and expensive-looking – so it was probably a tourist. All the better.

The car's headlights flicked to high beam then low again as it slowed almost to a halt. Ferguson chugged on.

The car's horn sounded, one bip, as if the driver thought that Ferguson hadn't seen the car.

'Reverse up the road,' Ferguson shouted, chugging to within ten feet of the car.

He heard a woman's voice, shouting something, and the car horn beeped three times in quick succession. Then the car started to reverse quickly as the harvester came alarmingly close.

Ferguson guessed he was only inches from the car when it started back, weaving back and forth across the road as the driver tried to reverse as fast as she could through the darkness.

Ferguson chuckled quietly to himself and accelerated, keeping as close to the car as he could, enjoying himself.

'Hurry up. Get out of my road.'

A couple of times – when he thought he might actually hit the car – he brushed his brake but the rest of the time he kept his foot firmly on the accelerator.

Five hundred yards back along the road, the woman reached a passing point and wrenched her car into it.

Ferguson swept past.

'Bloody city driver,' he shouted. 'Go back to Glasgow.'

He was still smiling when he swung through the gate in front of his cottage five minutes later. He felt good. He didn't analyse why he felt that way but it was as if he had offloaded some of his spite, managed to go a little way towards getting even with a rotten world in which wives walked out on you and people borrowed money and never paid it back and cows died for no reason.

Inside his cottage, he took a bottle of home-brewed beer from a cardboard box under the stairs and flicked the cap off by jamming it into the top of a drawer and twisting.

He took a swig straight from the bottle, strode into the lounge, turned on the television and flopped into a chair. He groaned and dragged himself to his feet when a quiz programme came on. Stamping back to the TV set he switched it on to another channel. A documentary – about the increase in the number of jobless.

'Lazy devils,' he muttered.

It was people like them who probably got most of the taxes he had to pay out of the pittance his farm earned. *He* was buying *their* TV sets, *their* beer, *their* cigarettes. There was just no justice.

'Some folk get it all their own way,' he grumbled, changing the channel again with an irritated jab of his finger. An old western came on, a John Wayne film. That would do to pass the time.

It was as he was sitting down again that he had the strange feeling that he was not alone, that someone was there with him.

Perhaps watching him?
Inside the house?
Or outside?

He looked over his shoulder, sweeping his eyes around the room.

No-one there.

He hauled himself to his feet, went to the window, cupped his hands around his eyes and pressed his nose against the glass.

He couldn't see much but he saw enough to know there was nothing out of the ordinary. Just the dim outline of the sheds and the barn, the caravan, the harvester, the car, the overgrown bushes nodding in the night breeze.

He snatched open the lounge door and flicked on the hall light.

Nothing. No-one there.

He was being foolish ...
And yet ...

He returned to his seat and swigged at his beer as John Wayne was marshalling his men behind some logs beside a

river. The distant war whoops of the Indians peeled through the room as he adjusted his cushion, settling in to wait for the Indians to attack.
Why did he feel uncomfortable?
Why ...
The camera panned across a wide river and reached a break in the trees at the far side just as the Indians burst into view, galloping into the water, kicking towards the other bank, rifles blazing.
There was tension in his shoulders.
Why?
Was there someone in the house? (*Don't be stupid,* he told himself. *Where do you get such foolish ideas? There's nothing in the house anyone would want to steal. Why should anyone bother to break in?*)
But the feeling wouldn't go away.
The Indians' ponies were being slowed down by the river now (why did they always attack across rivers where their ponies' lack of manoeuvrability made them sitting ducks?) and they were being flung out of their saddles by concerted rifle fire.
Creeeeeeeaaa.
A gentle rasping whisper.
The sound came from behind him.
Out in the hall.
No. Upstairs.
He sprang out of his seat and stared into the hall, his gaze taking in the bottom of the dark stairway. There was no denying that he had heard something.
It was ...
A door.
The groaning creak of a door.
Of course the wind would be to blame, wafting through some window he had forgotten to close, but he knew he wouldn't settle until he had searched the house, put his mind at rest.
Crossing the hall, he realised a pulse in his wrist had started to race, twitching rapidly under the skin.

He flicked on the light at the bottom of the stairs.
'Is somebody there?' he said quietly and his words seemed hollow as they rolled up the stairs.
Both bedroom doors were closed ...
therefore ...
therefore nothing.
It could have been the cupboard door or a wardrobe door.
The sound had definitely come from upstairs.
He was on the fifth step when he heard the sound again.
Creeeeeeeaaa.
Louder this time because ...
it came from under his own foot.
It was one of the stairs.
But how ...
Did that mean ...
It couldn't ...
He stared at the red stair-carpet under his right foot for a moment then continued to the top of the stairway, moving slowly, crouched, tensed.
'Who's there? Is someone ... '
His own voice, soft and breaking, alien in the stillness.
'Who's ... '
Then the bedroom door nearest to him was thrown violently open.

Three

When Ally Taggart appeared at the bedroom door, Ferguson yelped and jumped back, his heart thumping violently.

'What ... '

The young man's face was set in a broad grin, his eyes wide and wild, the pupils tiny pinpricks.

'Ally,' he gasped.

Taggart's hand jerked forward, a kitchen knife glinted and Ferguson felt a searing pain as the blade slid between his ribs.

He stumbled backwards, grabbed for the banisters, missed, and began to slump towards the floor, plucking desperately at the handle of the knife which protruded from his chest. He saw Taggart lunge at him again and a boot kicked him in the stomach. Then he was tumbling backwards down the stairs, going over and over.

Taggart sat on the top step impassively watching Ferguson convulsing in the pool of light at the bottom of the stairway, the circle of blood on the farmer's pullover growing larger and larger. When Ferguson was dead the youth stood up and walked slowly down the stairs.

He knew the patterns on the wallpaper beside his head were moving, each square quivering, each pastel-shade flower nodding its head, each coloured line trembling. His hand thrilled at the touch of the smooth banister. It seemed beautiful and warm and alive. Everything was alive. Nothing was as it had been before ...

Before ...

He screwed his face up but he couldn't remember *before*.

There was no *before*.

Only now.
Time was a trick.
A con.
Like everything else he had been told.
He stood over the corpse, looking into the pale face, the dead eyes.
Not dead.
Not really dead.
There was no such thing as alive or dead.
They were lies too.
Ferguson had been killed but he wasn't dead.
Why couldn't people see that?
Behind him, in the kitchen, he was aware that the tables and chairs were moving, the knives and forks rattling in the drawers, the geese on the wall calling to one another.
But that was all right, that was as it should be.
He knew that *now*.
He strolled into the lounge and found a very tall man there, wearing a cowboy hat, check shirt, leather waistcoat and jeans.
He said 'hello' to the man and the man said 'howdy'. That was when he realised it was John Wayne.
And Wayne had that knowing look that told Taggart that he too knew that fantasy and reality were one thing.
He talked to Taggart about 'injuns' and massacres and white settlers fighting back then folded his big frame into a chair and started to watch television.
Taggart was about to leave when he saw the box of matches. He picked it up, poked it open and took out a single match.
The red top whispered to him and he smiled.
He struck it on the box and stared at the flame as it flared. It was such a beautiful thing. Everything in the world was alive and gorgeous.
The flame ducked and bobbed and in its depths he could see a warm, red eternity.
'Tell me,' he said and it watched him for a long time, not doing anything, just teasing him, making him wait.

Suddenly, in the scarlet depths, he saw eyes and the flame stopped flickering and took on a definite outline.

The outline of a small man. The tiny figure was wearing a red jacket and trousers and the cheeky little face was topped by a mop of black hair.

Taggart knew he was one of the little people.

'Hello,' he said, and the tiny man ran along the match onto his hand, grinned up at him and started along the arm of his pullover, his feet sinking into the thick wool as if it was a snowdrift. He reached Taggart's elbow, took a deep breath and started to climb, his hands folding around thread after thread, his feet finding footholds in the pattern on the wool. When he reached Taggart's shoulder the young man could see sweat glistening on the tiny face.

The little man put his mouth close up to Taggart's ear and began to whisper.

And Taggart knew what it was he had to do.

Ten minutes later, Taggart was standing in the workshop at the rear of Macpherson's garage at the south end of Aragarr's High Street. His chest was heaving and he was bent double, his hands on his knees, trying to catch his breath after the long run from Ferguson's farm.

He had skirted the village and sprinted through the birch trees that ran along the far bank of the Aragarr Burn. Then he had splashed through the burn and swung through the field behind the cottages in Campbell Street, delighted at the fact that he had seen no-one and remained undetected.

As he had crept up behind the garage he had noticed that the little man who had come from the match was gone. But that didn't matter because he didn't need the little man anymore.

He had found one of the workshop windows slightly ajar, tugged it open and climbed in. The heaving in his chest eased and he stood upright and looked around him. The cars and the engines on the workbenches, the tools and the oily rags were all whispering to one another, talking about him. They knew why he had come. He giggled at the fact

that there was nothing they could do about it.
Nothing.
He crossed the dark workshop and found a jerrycan of petrol straight away.
Of course. It was right there waiting for him.
Then he opened the jerrycan and splashed petrol over the workbenches and half-dismantled engines and the seats of the cars.

He took an oily rag, climbed back through the window and lit the rag with the matches he had brought from Ferguson's farm.

Standing with his back pressed against the whitewashed wall of the workshop, he threw the smouldering rag through the window.

There was a loud whooooosh, as if a door had been opened on a hurricane, followed by several dull-thud explosions and flames shot through the window, lighting up the night.

As he turned to run, he saw a white face appear at the door of the Macphersons' house and recognised William Macpherson, the garage owner, a huge sixteen-stone giant of a man.

'Hey, I see you, I see who it is. Come back here.'

He heard the thump of Macpherson's feet above the roar of the fire as the big man came after him.

But he wasn't afraid.

He threw a glance over his shoulder and saw David MacPherson's face at an upstairs window. David was his age – nineteen – and they had gone to school together. He heard old Macpherson shouting 'David, call the fire brigade, somebody's torched the workshop. It's Ally Taggart. I'm going to get a hold of him.'

Taggart sprinted along Campbell Street, feeling as if he was flying.

What a thing.
To see flames shooting out of Macpherson's workshop.
Better than fireworks.

He could see the sea now, a grey-black shape sliced in two by a pillar of moonlight.

His feet skidded away from him at the corner of Campbell Street but he managed to stay upright, darted across the High Street and jumped down onto the beach.

'Come ... back ... you ... '

Macpherson's words came to him above the thump of the big man's feet. Then he heard other voices too, shouting, confused, and Macpherson yelling 'It's Ally Taggart ... he's set fire ... to my ... place.'

Taggart knew where he had to go, knew what he had to do.

He headed straight for The Rock, the stony promontory that jutted out from the beach and gave Aragarr its perfect harbour.

The thud of Macpherson's feet disappeared and Taggart realised the garage owner had reached the sand. He glanced back and saw that Macpherson had been joined by two other men, but in the dimness he couldn't make out who they were.

He started to laugh.

They thought they could catch him, but they couldn't.

And it was so funny because only he knew that.

He reached the promontory, jumped onto the first wet, shiny rock and began to climb, scrambling over boulder after boulder.

He paused when he reached the old path at the top and saw that Macpherson was well ahead of the other two men, climbing with angry, jerky movements.

A shrill giggle escaped from Taggart's lips.

He jogged away as Macpherson slithered over the last boulder.

'Come back ... here ... you ... '

Macpherson was only ten yards behind Taggart when the youth stopped the second time, whipping around to face his pursuers.

'You ... '

Macpherson seemed at a loss for words. He slowed to a quick walk, certain he had Taggart now, positive that Taggart had realised he couldn't escape.

'Why?' Macpherson yelled at the youth.

His face was twisted by exertion and anger as he reached a hand roughly towards Taggart's neck. He was surprised when Taggart knocked his hand away, shocked at the strength of a lad not much over ten stone. But he was even more surprised when he made his second grab for the youth. His hand brushed Taggart's shoulder and the body felt like metal beneath the jumper.

'What ... '

Taggart swung a savage punch which caught the big man on the side of the head and sent him flying back along the path, stumbling to his knees.

The other men were approaching when Taggart started to run again.

Oh, it was so funny.
They just didn't understand.

'William ... are you all right?' Voices behind him. A grunt from Macpherson as he was hauled to his feet.

Taggart looked back again when he reached a bend in the path and saw that there were other men behind the first three, a crowd of them, all chasing him, eager to help.

It didn't matter.
Didn't matter if there were a thousand.

He reached the end of the path, where it petered out on the top of a flat rock.

The last rock.

Beyond that there was only the naked cliff face, a two hundred feet drop to massive boulders covered in raging white water.

They thought they had him now.
But they didn't.

He jogged to the edge and turned to face them, his shoulders shaking with laughter.

There they were.
Fools.
Couldn't they see?
Even now.

He spun away, raised his arms above his head and leapt

off the edge.

What they didn't know was that he could fly.

A dozen faces watched from the clifftop as he fell, tumbling over and over, his laughter snatched away by the crash of the waves.

Then he was gone, his body punching through a fine mist and disappearing into a surge of white water.

THREE

The word was shrieked at McBaith as if by a crazy wild-haired witch.

He jerked awake and sat bolt upright in the bed of his London hotel, staring around him.

Three. Three. Three.

The word echoed around his brain, diminishing each time.

The Time of the Three had come ...

What did that mean?

His mind was filled with strange indistinguishable whisperings, as if a crowd of people were muttering to one another in a distant room.

It was beginning to happen ...
As it had been foretold.
He was fulfilling his destiny.
Going home.
Meant to ...

He shook his head, wiped sweat from his face and got out of bed.

A bad dream, that was all it was. One whisky too many on his flight ...

He shut out the whisperings and drank a glass of water.

Jetlag, he told himself as he got back into bed. *It was just jetlag.*

Four

Fiona Andrews woke with a start and sat up quickly, an odd elation coursing through her.

Why did she feel so good?

Her brow creased at the question.

She had been miserable since Ally Taggart had died yet now she felt so good.

Why?

She had been Taggart's girl-friend for almost a year. They had even spoken of marriage in that adolescent one-faraway-day-maybe-we'll-get-married kind of way. Then that terrible night had come along and the horrible day after – when the police had made it plain that they thought that Ally had done the things he had because he had become depressed after having an argument with her. His melancholy frame of mind combined with a large amount of whisky had tipped him over into a kind of drunken craziness, they had said.

She had cried for a day then sat mournfully at her window for another two, staring at the outside world and trying to make sense of the whole thing, trying to unravel the mystery of how life could be so impossibly cruel and how Ally (*shy, quiet Ally*) could have done the things everyone said he had.

I don't feel good, I feel great, she thought suddenly, analysing her mood.

It was as if all her youthful jauntiness and optimism had returned in one great surge, as if just being alive was exciting, thrilling, fascinating, as if she *knew* all her tomorrows held the promise of adventure.

It didn't make sense *but who cared.*

She swept back the blankets, threw off her nightgown, slipped into her underwear and tugged a brush through her tangle of red hair.

When she was satisfied with it, she dragged on a bulky-knit pullover and her favourite jeans – the ones that she had to struggle to get her hips into, the ones her mother didn't like because they were so tight but which Fiona liked because she knew they made the boys notice her (and that made her feel like she was really a woman and not just halfway there as her mother often told her).

She hopped on one leg as she pulled on the second of her black knee-boots and heard her mother shout: 'Is that you awake, Fiona?'

'Yes,' she yelled back.

As she went downstairs she thought of telling her mother how wonderful she felt but she decided not to. She knew her mother would just lecture her on how young girls' moods changed. Her mother was always talking to her like she was just a child, about moods and hormones and how young girls never knew their own minds. It was so annoying – she was eighteen after all, not twelve.

Her mother was putting cereal and orange juice on the kitchen table as Fiona entered the kitchen.

'How are you this morning?' her mother asked, folding plump arms across a floral apron and watching her in that way she always did, as if she was trying to read her mind, examine all her secrets.

'Fine, fine,' Fiona said non-committally.

'Will you be going in to work again today?'

She had had three days off after Taggart had died but had managed to get through yesterday at McCormack's shop where she worked.

'Yes, I will.'

'Good. Getting back to the normal routine is the only cure.'

'Yes.'

Her mother left the room, heading upstairs to make the beds, and Fiona sipped disinterestedly at her orange juice and stared out the window.

She could see there had been a shower of rain – one of those fine Aragarr drizzles – but it had stopped now and the street and the houses and The Rock were shining as if they had just been painted.

The world seemed oh-so beautiful to Fiona and the feeling of elation intensified, becoming a tingling sensation that ran through her body like a low-voltage electric current.

Then her eyes settled on a silver-coloured droplet of water hanging precariously from the wooden window frame.

She thought it looked like a diamond.

The bus plunged from shadows into brilliant sunshine as it reached the summit of the hill and started down the other side.

'Lovely day,' the driver said over his shoulder to Al McBaith who was seated in the front passenger seat, one of only two passengers on the bus. There had been ten but the numbers had dwindled as the bus made its way up the west coast of Scotland.

'Yeah.'

'We don't get many fine days at this time of the year,' the driver went on. 'I suppose we should look upon them as a kind of bonus to cheer us up before the winter comes.'

McBaith nodded. 'Winters bad up here, are they?'

'Aye, they can be, blizzards and such.'

McBaith craned his neck and leaned forward when he caught sight of the huge expanse of water away to his left.

'Loch Aragarr,' the driver said.

'I thought it must be.'

The loch was a beautiful grey-blue, the wind whipping up long white-topped ripples across its smooth back. It was about five hundred yards wide and McBaith could see where it reached the sea far to the west. He swung his head around but the eastern section of the loch was hidden by the shoulder of the hill. Between the road and the loch the ground fell away steeply, an exquisite tapestry of gold-leafed birch trees, grass, heather and naked grey boulders snuggling into the earth.

'The spot you want is just around the corner,' the driver said. 'Just beyond the top of this next hill.'

He gestured up ahead of him with his hand and McBaith nodded, climbed to his feet and began to stamp the stiffness out of his legs. As he lifted his suitcase out of the rack above his head he caught sight of the pine forest, regiment after regiment of trees lined up in close formation.

The driver dropped the bus down a gear as it began to chug up the steep hill, climbing through shadows. A minute or so later they crested the hill and the road swung to the right, parallel to the coast.

The driver pointed to his left and said: 'There ... there's Aragarr.'

McBaith hunched over and saw the village through a scattering of birch trees. Forty houses, maybe more, were crowded around a harbour which was sheltered by a huge outcrop of rock. Some of the houses were white and seemed to glitter in the sunshine but mostly they were grey – built of local stone, he had been told in a letter from Malcolm McBaith, his distant cousin God-only-knew how many times removed. Four fishing boats bobbed at their moorings in the harbour and there was a yellow speedboat which seemed out of place.

The driver braked to a halt when he reached the single-track road which ran down to Aragarr.

'Are you sure you want to get off here?' he said. 'As I told you before, we go right into the village.'

'No, here is just fine,' McBaith told him as the bus doors swished open.

He had decided on the spur of the moment when he had got onto the bus that he would get off at the top of the hill. Malcolm McBaith had told him how he could find his grandfather's cottage – or what was left of it – and he had decided to try to locate it before he went down into the village.

'Thanks again,' he shouted to the driver as the bus

pulled away, going down the hill.

He followed it, whistling between his teeth, the sun warm on his face.

So far his holiday had done him nothing but good. Constantly being in strange surroundings combined with the knowledge that he didn't have anything to do for three months but enjoy himself had given him a sense of freedom that he hadn't known for a long time. He had found London invigorating and lively, enjoyed the restaurants and pubs and tried out a startling variety of beers he had never heard of before. Although he wasn't much of a man for history he had decided that this was one occasion when he had to do the tourist bit. He had seen the Houses of Parliament, Westminster Abbey, the Tower of London and Nelson's Column, strolled along the Thames to see Cleopatra's Needle and visited three museums. He had enjoyed the sight-seeing more than he had expected to, finding satisfaction in each day on which he saw something unique.

The one thing he hadn't been prepared for was the startling variety of accents he encountered, particularly when he left London and travelled north on the train. And just when he was starting to think he had got the hang of them, his train crossed the border into Scotland and he found he had another array to contend with.

Four times since he had arrived at Gatwick the odd feeling that he had had on the plane had returned, the feeling that he was trapped in his destiny, simply moving along like an automaton, going to a place he knew. *Going home*. At first, he tried to analyse every facet of the weird sensation. It felt like time had slipped a cog, like every move he made was known in advance, written down in some little book which contained every street he would turn down, everything he would see, everything he would do, culminating with his visit to Aragarr.

It had started to climb into his mind a fifth time but he had rejected it irritatedly, kicked it away into a distant corner of his brain, forced himself to think about something else.

For prolonged periods too he had experienced that vague

fear that had been there for a month, like an anticipation of danger or an inexplicable sense of threat. It seemed to linger in his system like a mild hangover.

Halfway down the winding road to Aragarr, he found the break in the stone wall which ran along the south side of the road, just where Malcolm had said it would be in one of his letters. On one side of the opening the wall had collapsed but on the other he could see rusted iron fittings which had once supported a gate. He looked further down the road searching for another break in the wall but there wasn't one. This had to be the right place.

He slipped his suitcase down behind the wall, unwilling to carry it if he didn't have to, covered it with handfuls of weeds and grass, and started along the track beyond the break in the wall, studying the distant harbour and whistling the odd, melancholy tune that had been going around and around in his head for hours.

Idly, he tried to recall the name of the tune and where he had heard it. Had another passenger on the bus been whistling it? Had he overheard it on a radio somewhere? He couldn't find any answers. It seemed the tune had just popped into his mind and stayed.

He reached a point where the track split in two, one branch heading up the hill through a copse of birch trees, the other swinging west. He strode on without hesitation, taking the route west, then stopped dead.

Why had he been so sure this was the way? Malcolm had never mentioned the track splitting into two branches.

He looked around him.

Why had he felt a deep sense of familiarity with this place for the past few minutes, without even considering it? Why? Why did he feel that he was being ... *guided*.

Going home.

'Crap,' he said aloud and walked on. *Jesus, it was probably the wrong track.*

Then he came to two huge boulders set in the side of the hill, one in front of the other – the one highest up was huge and the second, at the other side of the track, was much smaller, like the child of the first.

He was wondering if this was the kind of stone which had been used to build most of the houses in Aragarr when he found himself in the broad clearing surrounded by birch trees.

And there it was. The cottage. The place where his grandfather had been born. He had come all the way back. Full circle.

There were four stone walls still standing, about two feet thick, he guessed, and some broad wooden beams which had once supported a roof. As he reached the empty doorway he saw the tall green weeds which had taken possession of the place, butting up through what had once been the floor.

He stepped inside and saw some kind of ridge along one wall, which he assumed had once been a shelf, a huge fireplace and one half of a stone chimney. He nodded slowly, letting his eyes roll over moss-covered walls, feeling the weeds nudging at his legs, moving in the wind which sighed through the vacant doorway and empty windows, and listening to the chattering of the birds in the birch trees – they seemed to be protesting at his presence.

He tried to imagine what the house had once been like, when people lived there, when his grandfather had been a child in ... When? The 1890s. At least there was a place still standing that was a part of his grandfather. Where would his children's children go if they had the inclination to look up something about their grandfather? What would there be left of Al McBaith except a couple of faded, dog-eared pictures? The thoughts led him to his eldest daughter, Alice. She had always been his favourite. Fourteen now and he hadn't seen her for a year and a half. How had things gone so wrong with him and Tina? Al would be seven now and Becky would be nine. *Dammit*.

Sometimes he thought life was like spending most of your time swimming underwater – you didn't see things clearly, everything was blurred, distorted. Occasionally, you came up for air, but each time a lot had changed and you couldn't quite figure out how.

He promised himself he would get over to Chicago and see Tina and the kids before he took up his new job in Oregon, even though it meant seeing Ron again. Tina's new husband was short, rich and fleshy with a smile that made him look like an ageing orang-outang and an urge to tell everyone his success story — even if they had heard it all before.

Suddenly a change came over the cottage, wiping away his thoughts. There was no physical change, no change in the wind or the sunlight or the chattering of the birds.

Yet something *had* happened.

It felt like a heaviness in the air, like the leaden atmosphere before a storm. It was as if each particle of air had drawn closer to its neighbour and they were squeezing against each other.

His skin tingled, feeling like drying cement, as he stepped outside, his eyes sweeping the clearing.

Everything looked the same and yet he knew something was different.

He compressed his lips and turned back into the cottage.

And that was when the word slipped into his brain, neat and sharp as a scalpel.

Four.

He stopped dead.

It wasn't as if the word had been spoken to him, it was as if it had jumped from his subconscious. Yet it had been a woman's voice — like the memory of what a woman had once said to him.

But what significance could ...

Then he remembered his first night in London and a word, shrieking in his mind, waking him up.

And that word had been *three.*

He was telling himself it was just one of those things that didn't mean anything when a sense of menace began to seep into him like slimy stagnant water.

A premonition of danger. Not here, but threatened.

An awareness of fear. Distant, like storm clouds gathering on the horizon.

The same sensation he had been experiencing for a month. Yet stronger now.

'Dammit,' he grunted. It was crazy. Old cottages and odd feelings didn't scare men like Al McBaith.

He shrugged the thoughts aside with a conscious effort and began to stroll about the cottage and clearing. Ten minutes later he decided it was time to go down to the village. He would return in a couple of days, he told himself, bring two or three cans of beer and just sit in the clearing and look at the view his grandfather must have looked at so often.

The heaviness in the air seemed to lift away instantly as he stepped out of the clearing onto the track and he turned back as if he expected to see something ... or someone.

But of course there was nothing there.

He whistled as he strolled back along the track – the same tune as before, slow, lilting, mournful, a tune that seemed to capture the essence of melancholy, or lost love or lost youth, or of an era and way of life which had passed and would never come again.

He reached the point where the track branched in two and headed back towards the road. He was walking in the shade of some birch trees when the branches parted in the wind and a shaft of sunlight penetrated, making him blink and turn his head away.

That was when he saw the woman, in the clearing away to his right, beyond the line of birches. He stopped and blinked again.

It was as if he was looking at a shot in one of those beautifully-filmed movies where the director might wait for days to get everything just right. She seemed to be framed perfectly between two birches, her fair hair tinted gold by the sun and the rusty reflection of leaves. The outline of her face and dress appeared filmy, indistinct, as if she was a dream image which might go *pop* and disappear if he took a step towards her.

She was standing side-on to him, studying something in her hands, and strands of hair had fallen over her face. Her dress was full-length and in a peasant style popular in the sixties and she was wearing sandals with cords which tied around her ankles.

She looks like a sixties hippy, McBaith thought, like someone transported out of her era in a time warp.

Suddenly it occurred to him that maybe he shouldn't be standing there staring at the woman, that maybe that was a little like being a Peeping Tom. In the instant that he started to turn away, she raised her head and smiled at him.

'I ... uh ... I'm sorry,' he heard himself say gruffly, too gruffly. He stepped forward through the trees, parting the branches with his arm.

'I didn't mean to stare at you. I hope I didn't scare you.'

'No, it's all right,' she said and her voice was soft and light.

He reached her and flashed his apologetic grin.

She had the palest of green eyes, he noticed, and they watched him in an almost childlike way, gazing at him with that look that some children have when they're staring at an object close up yet seem to be looking into the middle distance. The word *innocence* sprang into his mind. The face with its freckles and fine nose and slender lips seemed somehow devoid of guile, devoid of adulthood, open and dreamily carefree. Going by that face she could have been eighteen but there was something about her that said she was a woman not a girl, something ... and yet he couldn't put his finger on what it was.

She held up her hand and he saw that what she had been studying was a leaf.

'It's beautiful, isn't it?' she said.

'Yeah, I suppose it is.'

'Beautiful but very sad. I always think that when I see brown leaves. They're at the end of their cycle, rotting back into the earth again, going back to the beginning.'

He nodded slowly. 'I'd never really thought of it that way before.'

'Are you just visiting Aragarr?' she said.

'Uh-huh.'

Suddenly he realised that her accent wasn't like any of the array of accents he had encountered in Scotland.

'I'm new here myself,' she said as if reading his mind. 'I arrived two weeks ago from England.'

'What brought you up here?'

'I've rented a cottage ... I make jewellery for a living. I was looking for a place which would give me the solitude I long for.'

'You live alone?'

She nodded, smiling at him. 'Yes, as I said, I like being alone.'

'Me too,' he said, then he threw a glance at his watch and added, 'I've got to get moving. Maybe I'll see you around.'

'Yes.'

She smiled again as he raised his hand in a half wave and moved back through the trees.

'My name's Meg Rees,' she said.

'Al McBaith,' he shouted back, starting along the track.

Definitely an oddball, he thought as she disappeared from sight. Definitely not right. There was something too weird about her, too ... too *simple*. Maybe that was it? Maybe she was simple, had a screw loose?

Or maybe he was getting too old, too hardened? There was no rule that said everybody had to come from the same mould.

He shrugged, dismissing her from his thoughts as he reached the road, and went in search of his suitcase.

It was mad. How could it have happened? It made no sense at all.

Fiona Andrews stared down at the sea far below her as if seeking an explanation in the great waves which surged over huge boulders and butted into The Rock.

The place where Ally Taggart had been killed.

But what was she doing here? How had she got here?

She was on a slippery ledge, standing as rigid as a statue, and she felt as if her feet were welded to the wet stone.

She remembered serving the last customer at

McCormack's shop, saying good afternoon to Mr McCormack and stopping in the High Street to speak to Mrs Macpherson.

Then nothing.
How had she managed to get down onto this ledge?
Why?

The fact that there were no answers disturbed her, made her a little afraid, but she wasn't scared of falling. She knew that if she did slip she would ...

Fly. Yes, that was it. She would fly.

She began to giggle.

It would be wonderful to fly.

She stared at the huge yellow orb of the sun as it descended slowly across a blue, almost cloudless sky. It would be gone soon, ducking beneath the horizon. But it didn't matter. She knew that when the time came for her to fly she could follow it, exist forever in that magic place where the sun never set.

But there were things she had to do first.

Five

McBaith's Private Hotel stood at the top of an incline in Aragarr's High Street, opposite the sea-wall. If anybody was looking for Scottish seaside tranquillity, Al McBaith thought when he first saw it, this had to be it. The hotel looked out over the harbour and the long grey-black rocky promontory that seemed to protect it like a huge, gnarled hand. To the north, a light sea swell lapped at miles of empty beaches. Behind the hotel there appeared to be a small section of land given over to agriculture. Beyond that the ground rose steeply, all green grass and golden birches, to the main road and the pine forest.

The hotel itself was more like a large house than a hotel. It was built of grey stone and looked as if it had been recently sand-blasted clean. The windows were painted white and shone in the sunlight and there were window boxes full of flowers.

McBaith rang the doorbell and stepped inside. He found himself in a small, red-carpeted foyer. There was a desk and a cash till and a dining-room beyond. No people.

'*Anyone there?*' he shouted and his words seemed to echo through empty rooms.

'Anybody ... '

He had just started to shout a second time when he heard footsteps on the stairway. The man who appeared was small and wiry with a craggy face that could have belonged to a former lightweight boxer. His hair was grey and thinning. McBaith put him at about sixty. He had expected Malcom McBaith to be younger, about his own age.

'Malcolm?' he said.

'Al?'

'That's me.'

'Come in, come on in,' Malcolm said enthusiastically, thrusting out his hand. The handshake was firm, McBaith noticed, the hand hard and lean. He recalled that Malcolm had mentioned in one of his letters that he spent ten years as a fisherman before an uncle had left him enough money to buy the private hotel. Ten years at sea had left him with hands that didn't seem to belong on a hotelier.

Malcolm slid McBaith's suitcase behind the desk and led him into a large sitting-room.

'I was at the bus stop when the bus came in,' Malcolm said. 'When you weren't on it I thought I must have got the day wrong.'

'Hell,' McBaith groaned, 'I didn't think you'd do that. I got off at the top of the hill and went to see my grandfather's cottage.'

'Oh never mind that now. You'll have a dram ... a whisky? Or maybe you would prefer a beer?'

'Whisky'll be OK.'

Malcolm hurried out of the room and returned a moment later with two glasses on a tray.

'Where is everybody?' McBaith said.

'Everybody?'

'Your guests.'

'It's very seasonal in Aragarr. I make my living in the tourist season. This is off-season. You've got the run of the place. No other guests at all. I hope you weren't expecting the Aragarr Hilton.'

McBaith laughed. 'No.'

'I only keep the place open at this time of year because I live here and we do get occasional bookings from people silly enough to want to come here when it's cold. Now tell me how was your trip?'

'Just great.'

They talked for two hours with never a lull in the conversation, discussing the US branch of the McBaiths, California, the McBaiths of Aragarr ('There were more than a score of us here once,' Malcolm said, 'but now there's only me.'), the waxing and waning fortunes of the Aragarr fishing fleet (now down to only four boats), the village's growing dependence on tourism, the 'folk who buy our houses as holiday homes', the 'outsiders' who had come in to start up cottage industries (McBaith thought of Meg Rees but didn't mention her), and a score of other topics.

McBaith found himself studying Malcolm's gestures, searching the older man's face for some family resemblance, something that was distinctly *McBaith*, and he was a little disappointed when he didn't find anything. Then he realised they had one trait in common – they were both *talkers*, most at home when they were spinning yarns and embellishing them a little (or at least it was a little in McBaith's case – he suspected some of Malcolm's tales about life at sea were ten per cent truth, ninety per cent fisherman's invention).

Half an hour after he met Malcolm in the foyer, McBaith began to suspect something was wrong. At first he couldn't put his finger on why he felt that, yet as the conversation continued the same notion kept coming back to him. There was a strain in Malcolm's eyes, a tenseness around his mouth and occasional fidgeting gestures that betrayed ... *something*.

He found out what it was when they were having their evening meal (Malcolm called it tea) in a small room off the main dining-room. 'A piece of fish like you've never tasted,' Malcolm had promised. 'I got it myself from Sandy McLeod, fresh from the hold of the Homecoming.' His boast hadn't been far off the mark, McBaith had to concede when he tasted the haddock in its mushroom sauce.

The room was filled with a memorabilia of a man's life – rows of books, a picture of a man in uniform which McBaith supposed was Malcolm, a fisherman's thick woollen hat hanging on a peg, a row of medals in a display case, a painting of the hotel as it had been in 1905 and a black and white picture of a boy about ten years old.

It was when McBaith said, 'Your son?' nodding to the picture, that he knew he had stumbled onto what was troubling the older man.

'No,' Malcolm sighed. 'I never married. That's my nephew.'

McBaith nodded slowly and there was a pause in which Malcolm cleared his throat and dropped his eyes away from McBaith for a moment.

When he raised his head again, he said, 'That's Ally. He was my younger sister's boy. She married a John Taggart and moved to Glasgow. She and John were killed in a car crash and I brought the boy up. That's an old picture of course ... Ally was nineteen when ... '

Malcolm stopped abruptly, seeming to run out of words. McBaith didn't say anything. He tried not to look at Malcolm, whose face was set now, the muscles tight, as if he was afraid he might betray emotion.

'He was killed a few days ago,' he said suddenly, quickly, as if eager to speak the words and get it over and done with.

'Killed?'

'Aye.'

'How?'

'It's not something I feel like talking about just now.'

McBaith gestured apologetically. 'Sorry,' he said, 'I didn't mean to poke my nose into your business.'

Malcolm started to clear the table, gripping McBaith's arm as he passed behind him. 'It's not that, laddie. I'm just not ready to talk about it yet. The time's not right.'

McBaith noticed that Malcolm's lower lip was quivering as he carried the dishes into the kitchen but the older man's face was under control when he returned.

'Do you know what you should do tonight,' he said.

'No what?'

'Take a walk along the harbour. It's pretty at night at this time of the year when all the street lights are on and the moon is out. There's a pub, you know – the Jacobite Arms. You could have a drink there and ... '

'Are you coming?'

'I haven't been out much since Ally died. As I said before, I'm not ready yet. Not ready to meet people and talk about it. But you should go. There are a lot of folk in the village know that you're coming. I'm sure they'd like to meet you and hear all about America. I'll show you your room now if you like. You might want a bath before you go out ... the bathroom's at the end of the hall upstairs.'

McBaith stood up. 'You go ahead and do the dishes. I'll find the room myself. Which one is it?'

'Top of the stairs, first right. The key's in the door. If you don't fancy the view just pick any room you like.'

McBaith started to turn away then swung back. 'It's been great meeting you today, Malcolm. I hope I'm not putting you to any trouble.'

'Of course not. You're a McBaith, aren't you?'

'There is one thing I'd like to get sorted out,' McBaith said. 'You said in your letter that you wouldn't take any money from me for staying here. I understand that as a sentiment but you're running a business and I ... '

'I'll not take a penny,' Malcolm smiled.

'You'll have to let me throw in a couple of hundred dollars towards the cost of my food and ... '

Malcolm shook his head. 'Not a penny,' he said and turned into the kitchen with an armful of dishes.

His head reappeared a moment later and he grinned at McBaith. 'I'll not say no if you bring a bottle of Grouse into the house,' he said.

'It's a deal,' McBaith said.

He fetched the suitcase and climbed the narrow stairway to his room on the first floor. It was small but clean and comfortable and the view of the moonlit harbour and sea and High Street was splendid.

McBaith unpacked his suitcase, grabbed a towel and headed for the bathroom. He was disappointed there was no shower but the bath was huge – unlike many baths he had encountered it managed to accommodate even his large frame.

When he had dressed again – in jeans, heavy pullover and check sports jacket – he went downstairs whistling softly to himself and found Malcolm in the kitchen.

The older man handed him a whisky, poured one for himself, and looked at him with a question in his eyes.

'Something wrong?' McBaith said.

'That tune ... '

'What?'

'The one you were whistling.'

'What about it?'

'Where did you hear it?'

'I was thinking about that myself this afternoon. It's been going around and around in my head all day. Dunno how I heard it. Why? What's wrong with it?'

'It's just that I haven't heard it in years.'

'You know it?'

Malcolm sipped at his whisky. 'Oh aye. It's an old Aragarr tune. I never hear it nowadays but there was a time when I was a lad when the older folk used to sing it and whistle it. I've no idea what it's called. Perhaps you heard it from your grandfather?'

'Yeah,' McBaith said. 'I guess you must be right.'

Douglas Renfrew cursed the puncture that had flattened the front tyre of his bicycle with an eloquence that many fishermen possess and plunged the black tube in his hands into a bucket of water, his eyes searching the surface for any sign of bubbles. There were none and he shifted the tube through his fingers.

There wasn't much light in the shed at the back of his house three doors away from McBaith's Private Hotel but his wife, Margery, had turned down his suggestion that he mend the puncture in *her* kitchen with a contemptuous, almost threatening glance. What light there was in the shed came from an old oil lamp that stood on top of the cobwebbed desk he was kneeling in front of – the desk on which he had done his homework as a schoolboy forty years before.

He continued to slide the tube through his fingers, cursing the cold water, the lack of tell-tale bubbles and his wife's failure to be more understanding.

After all, it wasn't as if he could put off repairing the puncture. He had to have the bike ready for first thing in the morning because he had to be in Kinallach by eight-thirty and that was five miles away. There was a car he wanted to buy from Tommy Ross and Ross had said he could have first refusal. 'It's a steal at five hundred,' Ross had told Renfrew, 'but somebody else is coming to see it at nine o'clock. You get here first, put your money on the table and it's yours.' He had been waiting for three months for Ross to come up with a cheap car that still had a lot of mileage left in it and was determined not to miss the opportunity.

The concrete floor was cold and a chill began to gnaw its way into his knees and climb slowly up through his thighs.

It was as he shifted his knees further apart, into a more comfortable position, that he saw the bubbles pop to the top of the water.

There it was. He drew the inner tube out of the water.

And in that instant the source of light in the shed moved.

He jerked his head up and stared at the lamp. It stood in the far corner of the shed now, emitting the same yellow glow as before.

But it had moved, all of six feet.

He lowered his head and studied the tube.

Of course the lamp hadn't moved. It couldn't just move therefore it hadn't. Inanimate objects couldn't move of their own accord.

His mind scampered around the subject, desperate to shut out all thoughts about the lamp, grabbing for normality, denying the evidence of his own eyes.

He dabbed chalk on the puncture and began to dry the area around the hole with a cloth.

But the lamp had moved. It had ...

Suddenly it was back.

There. Just a few feet away. On the desk.

He froze, staring up at the lamp, like a man kneeling in a cathedral who has just received a stunning revelation. A nerve end twitched at the corner of his mouth and something quivered down his spine.

Of course it had never moved in the first place.
Why had he thought it had?
What was happening to him?
He was seeing things, imagining things that couldn't possibly be occurring.
Did this kind of thing happen to everyone? Was it just the mind playing a trick?
It was daft whatever it was, he decided, and began to imagine what Margery would say if he told her. An uneasy grin creased his face.
That's it – *laugh*. Laugh because it hadn't actually happened. There wasn't even a shelf for the lamp to stand on in the corner of the shed, he reminded himself. There was nothing there, just two walls and empty space.
He reached for the rubber repair patch, removed the adhesive paper from the back and carefully pressed the patch over the puncture, holding it firmly in place with his thumb.
Then he heard a faint scraping noise and knew the lamp had gone again, across the room into the corner.
There was a dimness in front of him now, while before the light had shone directly onto his hands. Now the glow was away to his right.
But ...
It could not be.
He didn't raise his head this time, didn't turn towards the lamp. He just held the rubber patch firmly in place until he was certain it was stuck there.
I'll put the tube back in the tyre and pump it up in the morning, he told himself. *No point in doing it now. No point in ...*
He was scared, trying to get away.
Scared of a lamp that couldn't have ...
But had.
He noticed his fingers were trembling.
In God's name this is foolishness, a voice in his head seemed to be telling him. He wouldn't run away, he would put the tube back in the tyre and pump it up just as he had planned to.

'God,' he breathed as the scraping sound came again and the lamp glow fell over his hands.

Back on the desk.

He swallowed and stood up stiffly, letting his eyes slide towards the lamp.

There it was, just where it always was, just where it had been when he had lit it.

He chuckled but it was an uneasy, uncertain chuckle, like a child whistling in the dark to mask his fear.

A mind trick, that was all it was. Like the tricks your mind played when you were dreaming and woke up halfway through the dream and still thought you were being chased through a dark forest by a man with no face.

All the same he found that he desperately wanted to be inside the house with his feet up in front of the blazing fire, Margery chattering, the television blaring in the corner.

Wanted to be anywhere but in that shed.

He hesitated then leaned forward and began to turn the lamp off. There was no warmth in it, he noticed. It was ice cold, as if it had been left out overnight in the snow.

It shouldn't be cold. It shouldn't ...

The flame flickered and died and he snatched open the door and cursed at the slender shafts of panic that seared through him as his jacket became entangled in the bike's handlebars. He managed to jerk it free and stumbled outside, letting the door swing closed behind him.

Halfway across the dark yard, his eyes picked up a faint glow, coming from behind him, and he spun around.

Light was bleeding around the edges of the ill-fitting door.

The lamp had come on again.

Impossible. He had turned the switch all the way round.

Something that felt like a frosty blanket lightly caressed his back.

Then the light flickered, intensifying to the right of the door, diminishing to the left.

The lamp was moving again.

He swallowed with difficulty, spun away and hurried to

his back door where he forced himself to look at the shed once again.

The light was fading now, growing dimmer and dimmer as if the lamp switch was being slowly turned down by an invisible hand.

Then it was gone. What he was staring at was a dark shed just like any other shed.

It was as his hand folded over the doorknob that he remembered something.

Remembered that when he had been a child there had been a shelf in that corner of the shed. In his grandfather's day that was where the lamp had always stood.

But the shelf hadn't been there for fifty years.

Six

Killed, Al McBaith thought as he strolled along the High Street through the pools of weak light that hung around the street lamps. *Killed.* He gazed absently at the stealthily-shifting sea beyond the harbour wall and let the word idle around in his brain. It was the word Malcolm had used. *His nephew had been killed.*

McBaith wondered what could have claimed the life of a nineteen-year-old boy. A car accident? A tragedy at sea? A fall from a motorcycle? If it had been one of those terrible diseases with long and unpronounceable names Malcolm would have been more likely to use the word *died*. But he had said *killed*.

I'm still thinking like a cop, he told himself, but old habits died hard and anyway it was the kind of thing that would make anyone prick their ears up.

He reached the towering rocky promontory at the end of the harbour – which Malcolm had told him was called The Rock – then turned back and headed for the Jacobite Arms.

As he approached the pub, sounds washed over him – the clinking of glasses, a woman's laugh, men's voices – and he saw smoke leaking from two windows and rising into the night air.

There were two bars and he hesitated outside, looking from one door to the other. On the frosted-glass upper half of the first door, in ornate black writing, were the words 'Jacobite Arms'; on the second the word 'Lounge'.

He chose the lounge and went inside. There were about a dozen people there and he felt eyes studying him as he strolled across the room. Malcolm had said tourism was seasonal in Aragarr and this was off-season and he guessed that explained the interest. There probably weren't many strangers around at this time of year.

The barmaid was plump, pretty and forty and had left one blouse button too many undone, exposing an immense cleavage. She flashed him a big smile.

'Lager,' he said and threw a glance into the other bar. He saw two men playing darts and a vacant pool table.

'Pint?' she said and he gestured with thumb and index finger that something smaller would do.

'Half?'

'Yeah, that'll do.'

'You're an American, aren't you?' she said, tugging at the lager tap.

'You guessed.'

'We don't get many Americans in Aragarr.'

'What about tourists?'

'Mostly English ... and Germans.'

'I heard you had a lot of American oilmen in Scotland these days.'

'Not in Aragarr ... no oil rigs here.'

She took the pound note out of his hand and fetched his change.

'All Americans sound like actors to me.'

'Do they?'

She took a step back and studied his face as if it was an interesting sculpture in an art gallery.

'You look a bit like an actor.'

'Which one? Redford like he was as the "Sundance Kid"?'

'No ... the other one ... he's made lots of pictures.'

'Newman?' he grinned.

'No ... in that war picture.'

'John Wayne? Humphrey Bogart?'

'No.'

He chuckled. 'Peter Lorre?'

'No.'

'Gene Hackman?'

'No.'
'Give up.'
'It'll come to me,' she said, turning to another customer who had moved over to the bar.
'Another pint for me, Liz,' the man said, then turned and looked frankly at McBaith.
After a moment, he said: 'You'll be McBaith, the one from America.'
'That's right.'
The man was as tall as McBaith but gaunt, his seamed, aged face topped by unruly grey hair.
'Neil Ritchie,' he said and they shook hands. 'When did you arrive?'
'A couple of hours ago.'
'Is Malcolm coming along for a drink?'
'No.'
Ritchie shook his head slowly, with exaggerated sadness.
'Oh,' he said. 'A shame. He hasn't been here since ... well, you've probably heard.'
'Since his nephew was killed?'
'Aye, a terrible, terrible thing.'
McBaith sipped his beer.
'Car accident?' he said.
'What?' Ritchie looked confused.
'Was it a car accident?'
'You mean Malcolm didn't tell you?'
'He seemed pretty cut up about it, didn't feel like talking.'
'No,' Ritchie said quietly, 'it was no car accident.'
'Well, what happened?'
'He killed a man ... ' Ritchie said.
'Killed a man,' McBaith repeated. He hadn't thought of Aragarr as the kind of place likely to have a high crime rate and his surprise showed in his voice.
'Aye, and there's more.'
Ritchie outlined as much as he knew from village gossip about the night when Taggart had killed Brian Ferguson, set fire to Macpherson's workshop and leapt to his death.

He leaned close up to McBaith as he spoke, as if he was divulging something top secret, but McBaith noticed the conversation in the lounge had died down and knew people were listening.

'I don't get it,' McBaith said just as a voice from the other end of the room shouted, 'Neil'.

Ritchie spun around and flicked his head questioningly.

A powerfully-built man in his middle-fifties, who was seated with a group of seven or eight people, was beckoning to Ritchie.

'Is that the other McBaith?' he shouted, warming his hands over a crackling log in an open fireplace then rubbing them together.

'It is,' said Ritchie.

'Well, don't keep him all to yourself, bring him over.'

Ritchie's eyebrows raised in an invitation. 'Would you join us, Mr McBaith?'

'I'd be glad to ... and call me Al.'

There were men and women in the group seated by the fire, old, young and middle-aged. A solid cross-section of the population, McBaith thought. But there was only one he really noticed. When Ritchie reached her in his round of introductions ('Al McBaith, this is Janet, my niece. Janet is the teacher here in Aragarr.') McBaith's eyes took in a face that seemed to be a mass of fascinating contradictions, rebellious and tranquil at the same time. The wide, full-lipped mouth didn't seem to go with the fragile curve of her chin and the nose appeared slightly too large, too arrogant, too masculine to be at home with the watchful eyes which were of the palest, powdery blue. The silky black, shoulder length hair and the dark eyebrows seemed at odds with her fair skin. But despite all the contradictions – or perhaps because of them – he found her incredibly beautiful.

The edge of her mouth tugged itself up into an amused half-smile as he nodded to her and said: 'Hi, nice to meet you.'

The eyes held his just too long for there to be any doubt that she found him attractive.

(*Come-on eyes*, he thought. *Aragarr is full of surprises.*)

'I was just telling Mr McBaith what happened to Ally Taggart,' Ritchie said.

'It was a shock to us all,' one woman said. McBaith looked at her. She was about fifty without a trace of grey in her curly blonde hair and he guessed she dyed it. 'It's still hard to believe that it really happened.'

'And he actually *jumped* off the cliff?' McBaith said.

'Aye,' said the big man who had called them over – Ritchie had said his name was Macpherson. 'And he was laughing.'

'Laughing.'

'That's right. He just laughed at all of us ... then turned and jumped, as if he was diving into a swimming-pool.'

McBaith turned to Ritchie. 'How do you know that he killed this farmer ... Ferguson?'

'Well, he was covered in blood, you see,' Ritchie said.

'Covered in the stuff,' Macpherson interrupted. 'It was my workshop he set on fire. I chased him out to the end of The Rock. His clothes and shoes were soaked in blood.'

'Did he have some kind of grudge against Ferguson?'

The blonde woman gave a kind of sniggering half-laugh and said: 'Everybody had a grudge against Ferguson, if you believed what Ferguson said. He had a chip on his shoulder and he wasn't the friendliest man in Aragarr.'

'He wasn't very popular,' Ritchie conceded. 'Not that he was a bad man, mind you. I always thought he was a kind of sad ... sad and lonely man. It's true that he wasn't easy to get along with.'

McBaith looked at Macpherson. 'What did Taggart have against you?' he asked just as it occurred to him that all his questions were making him sound like a cop.

Macpherson shrugged. 'I have no idea. He was a pal of my son's. I knew him quite well, always got on all right with him ... he was a quiet boy. I don't think anybody really knew him all that well except maybe for Malcolm. Oh, and his girl-friend, Fiona.'

'You're right when you say Ally was quiet, and that's

why it just doesn't make sense,' said the blonde woman. 'Ally was such a nice boy, such a fine boy. Shy, you know. This is not the kind of thing you think is possible from a boy like Ally.'

'What do the police say?' McBaith said.

'Och, they've got it all worked out,' Ritchie said. 'They say he had a fight with his girl-friend, got himself good and drunk and went out of his mind. They say Ferguson said or did something to offend him and he killed Ferguson in a drunken rage – probably didn't know what he was doing, the police think.'

'What do you think?'

Ritchie pursed his lips. 'It's a bit of a mystery right enough but the police are probably right. That's what they're paid for. They don't tell me how to haul in my nets ... and I don't tell them how to do their job.'

'Maybe Mr McBaith has other ideas,' Janet Ritchie said and when McBaith glanced at her the blue eyes met his, unwavering, the amused half-smile tugging at her mouth again. 'Mr McBaith is a policeman himself.'

'The name's Al and I'm not a police officer any more.'

'But what do you think?' Ritchie said.

'Was there an autopsy on the body?' McBaith asked. 'A post-mortem.'

'There is no body,' Janet said. 'The body hasn't been recovered yet.'

McBaith found himself looking into those blue eyes again and they seemed so inviting, carrying on a wordless conversation with his. For a flickering instant, they seemed familiar, as if he had known her somewhere before, but he knew that was impossible.

He nodded slowly as the blonde said: 'The sea just carried him off. He'll be washed up one of these days ... on some beach ... or in Ireland maybe.'

'Why?' Ritchie said. 'What is it you think a post-mortem would find? Do you have something in mind?'

McBaith shrugged. 'I'm not sure,' he said. None of this was really his business. He knew bar-room speculation and guess-work never got anyone anywhere.'

'If you have something in mind, please let us in on it,' Janet said.

Those blue eyes again – he felt they were reading his thoughts now. He shifted his gaze to Macpherson.

'You say the kid was covered in blood, laughing and jumped off the cliff deliberately.'

'Aye ... he was like a lunatic.'

'Anything else unusual about him?'

Macpherson thought a moment then said: 'Yes ... there was. He knocked me down for one thing ... a boy not half my size. And his body was hard ... '

'Hard?'

'Really hard ... hard as stone.'

'What is it you have on your mind, Al?' Janet said.

'I ... I'm not sure I should butt in.'

'You're not considering the possibility of drugs?' she said.

'It had crossed my mind.'

'The police thought of that too.'

'I guessed they would.'

'The thing is,' Janet said, 'there are no drugs in Aragarr.'

'I thought they were everywhere now.'

'This is not downtown Los Angeles,' Ritchie said stiffly and McBaith wished he had kept his opinions to himself. He didn't want to step on any toes on his first day in Aragarr.

Suddenly an old woman seated beside the fire stabbed a finger in McBaith's direction. Throughout the conversation, she had been silent, warming her hands over the flames which leapt from the log, her damp, grey eyes watching McBaith placidly.

'You were wrong to think there were drugs in Aragarr,' she said, 'but the police were wrong too.' McBaith looked at her – unkempt grey hair camped on top of a square, wrinkled face, leathery skin tight over the bones. 'Ally wasn't on drugs,' she continued, 'but it wasn't the drink that did it either. The trouble is people are looking for the answer in the world of men ... and you won't find the answer in the world of men.'

'What d'you mean?' McBaith said.

'Oh, be quiet, Annie,' Ritchie said. 'You're just an old fool.'

'Old I may be, but I'm no fool. Mark my words ... you won't find the answer in the world of men. Too much has been happening.'

'What ... ' McBaith began but then Ritchie caught his eye and gave him the kind of look that barmen give customers to tell them that they've been trapped into a conversation with the bar drunk, the town's number one earbender.

'Just ignore her,' Macpherson said. 'If you listen to Annie Stewart and believe every word she says you'll end up thinking she has the wisdom of Solomon and knows all the secrets of the universe.'

Annie grunted and turned her face back to the fire. 'It's such a shame,' the blonde said after an embarrassed pause in the conversation. 'Mr McBaith has just arrived from America and what do we greet him with on his first day in Aragarr ... nothing but stories of tragedy. What happened to Ally is over and done with, there's nothing can bring the boy back. Let's have a little laughter, a good story or two. Tell me, Mr McBaith, what is America like?'

Fiona Andrews blinked her eyes open and stared at the ceiling in her dim bedroom. The only light in the room was from the street lamp outside – it was not yellow, it was weak and colourless, without substance. After a moment she turned her head and stared at the point where the light trickled between half-open curtains.

The light was beckoning to her, trying to tell her something. She knew that ...

But what?

What was it trying to say?

Then she remembered the place where she was going to go soon, the place where it was always warm and where the sun never set.

Maybe it was time to do the things she had to do.

The curtain bulged as if a hand had pushed in through the window (but it was only the wind of course) and the light fell over her face.

And the light was *warm*. It made her feel so good. And it spoke to her.

She smiled at it and thought for a moment she saw Ally's face in the weak glow, then she got out of bed, dragged her nightgown over her head and dressed in jeans, heavy pullover and running shoes.

She had to wear running shoes because she would have to be very quiet if she was to do what the light had told her and get back to her bed undetected.

She tiptoed to the door and paused, her head cocked to one side, listening for any sounds coming from the bedroom next door or from the rooms downstairs. She knew her parents would probably be in bed, but would they be asleep?

She heard nothing and crept along the upstairs hall, keeping to the carpet, avoiding the polished wood at either side. A giggle forced its way up from her throat and she clamped her hands over her mouth, trapping it there. The door to her parents' bedroom was slightly ajar and she stood outside for several seconds, listening to their rhythmic sleep-breathing.

Satisfied, she hurried downstairs, careful to step over the third-bottom step – the one which always creaked – and went into the kitchen.

She found her father's lighter on the table and the penknife in a drawer and shoved both items into the pockets of her jeans. Then she opened a cupboard and felt around in the dark until her hand encountered a pile of old newspapers. She picked up three or four, stuffed them under her pullover, and let herself out the front door.

Shivering, she walked quickly along the High Street, keeping in the shadows where she could, her eyes darting about, her ears straining for any sign of human activity.

She knew it was important that nobody saw her and that

she managed to do what the voice in the light told her without being found out. She knew there would be other tasks to perform before she received her reward.

She reached the white, two-storey house at the corner of Gordon Street, tiptoed down the side and stepped over the small gate into the garden. There were no lights on in the house and she found the unlocked window immediately – just as she had known she would.

Gently, she drew it open, pausing only once when the ageing window frame groaned. Then she climbed inside, slid across a damp sink, and stood in the centre of the dark kitchen, listening.

She heard a clock ticking. The sound of her own shallow breathing. Nothing else.

Perfect.

She stepped silently into the lounge, took out the penknife and began to attack the settee, stabbing and slicing at it again and again. It felt pleasant, ripping and tearing at the fabric. Finally it was in shreds, stuffing scattered all around her. She paused, panting, listening to the silent house. Nothing. Everything was going perfectly.

She rushed across the room and slashed open the two easy chairs. Then she took the newspapers from under her pullover, screwed them up and stuffed them into the settee and the chairs.

That was the lounge finished, she thought, now for the kitchen. She hurried through the door, found the gas cooker, and turned the control all the way round. The hiss of gas subdued the tick-tock of the clock.

She returned to the lounge and stood with her hands on her hips, surveying the room. Beautiful. It was going to work perfectly. What a sight it would be. The voice in the light would be so pleased.

She was enjoying herself so much she was reluctant to take the next step – the last step. She didn't want her fun to end.

But it had to be done.

She took out the lighter, flicked it on and held it up in

front of her face, staring into the blue-yellow flame. Of course it wasn't just a flame, though it might have appeared to be that to anyone else – it was the light, an eternity of light, an entire universe, a place where the sun never set.

She sighed, bent forward and held the flame against a corner of a newspaper which protruded from the settee. The flame licked hungrily over the paper and she moved the lighter to another piece of paper, then another. By the time she had finished with the settee a score of yellow flames were darting out of it and pillars of grey smoke were dribbling towards the ceiling. She set fire to the easy chairs then held the lighter under the curtains and watched orange tongues of flame shooting up, scorching the wall.

Standing in the centre of the room, she watched the blaze grow until the smoke biting at her throat made her cough. Then she unlocked the front door, checked there was no one in the street and stepped into the front garden.

Seven

It was just after ten-thirty when McBaith left the Jacobite Arms. As he was going out the door, Liz, the barmaid, who was shining a glass vigorously, shouted after him: 'I've remembered.'

'Remembered what?' he said, holding the door half open, the cold night air washing over him.

'Remembered which actor it is you remind me of. I knew I would. I said it would come to me.'

'Who?' he said, smiling good-naturedly.

'George C. Scott,' she said with a note of triumph in her voice. 'He was in "Patton" and ... '

'Yeah, I know who George C. Scott is.'

'The face and the way you move ... just like him. Hasn't anyone ever told you that before?'

'No, I can't say they have.'

'It's true. I'm not pulling your leg.'

He chuckled as he went out the door. *George C. Scott.* He guessed he could live with looking like George C. Scott but it was funny nobody had ever noticed that before. Probably because the whole thing was a barmaid's fantasy.

A chill wind whipped at his waterproof jacket as he stepped into the street and he zipped it up and turned up the collar.

He had taken no more than half a dozen steps when he smelled smoke.

The odour bit into his nostrils, harsh and acrid. This was no woodfire or smoky chimney. Instantly he was sure of that.

He stopped, turned slowly and saw the fire immediately. Ugly, dark-grey fingers of smoke were curling under the bottom of a slightly-open window and trailing away into the night. Through the window he saw flames flickering against a backdrop of billowing smoke.

Three running strides took him back to the pub. He threw the door open and yelled at the barmaid.

'There's a fire a couple of houses down the road. Call the fire department and get help.'

As he spun away he was vaguely aware that people were rushing across the lounge towards him, eager to help.

It was as he started to jog towards the house that he saw a figure in dark clothes running away down the street, dodging the pools of light from the street lamps, trying to stay in the darkest places.

Why?

It looked suspicious but surely this was someone running for help.

But *no* – he rejected that immediately. If this person was looking for help he or she would have headed for the pub. That was the obvious place to raise the alarm. Why run *away* from the centre of the village?

He reached the house, aware of the thud of running feet and voices raised in concern behind him – 'It's the McLeod place' ... 'Is Liz calling the fire brigade?' ... 'Somebody get a ladder, Mrs McLeod sleeps upstairs ... '

He hesitated but didn't stop. His pace faltered then he kicked on, chasing the figure who was now about fifty yards away.

The figure appeared to slow down and disappear from sight. Then McBaith saw a face – a pale blot in the darkness – peering out at him from a doorway. Whoever it was had tried to hide there.

He shouted 'Hey' and the figure leapt forward, spun away from him and started running again.

A girl. He was sure it was a girl. He had seen a flash of long reddish hair and there was something about the way she ran.

McBaith was panting now, the beer he had drunk heavy in his stomach.

Why was she running away? Had she started the fire? She was acting suspiciously but ...

He flung the thoughts aside and shouted again. 'Hold on there ... Hey ... ' Her hair swung out behind her as she dashed into a dark lane – no more than ten yards ahead of him now – and disappeared from view.

He kicked harder and whipped into the lane, bumping his shoulder on a wall.

There she was, a girl of about eighteen. She was climbing a picket fence and for an instant her face was turned towards him, glimpsed clearly in the lights from the High Street. The muscles of her face were visibly quivering under the skin and the violently twitching mouth and staring eyes gave her a haunted expression that seemed to be made up of an equal mixture of horror and uncontrollable fury.

'Hold it ... you can't get away ... what ... '

She cleared the fence as he reached it and he lunged at her, grabbing over the fence, his fingers grasping a handful of a woolly pullover.

She swung around instantly and slapped at him with an open hand. The force of the blow took him by surprise and he felt himself falling sideways, his elbow jarring into the fence.

Usually it would have taken a heavyweight to knock him off balance and this was just a smallish teenage girl – it didn't make sense – but as his mind scrambled for answers he put it down to the fact that he must have been off balance anyway, stretching over the fence as he was.

Suddenly a great *keeeeeraaaaaaak* ravaged through the night, a not-too-distant explosion. It sounded like the blast of a shell or a grenade going off in a confined space.

McBaith jumped, startled, but held on, twisting the pullover around his fist and dragging the girl backwards as he pushed himself upright.

'Cut it out,' he yelled as she hit him again, a fingernail jabbing into his eye this time.

She screamed then – 'Nooooo' – a scream that went right through him the same way a fingernail scraping on a blackboard might have, a scream of anguish and intense fury.

'Listen ... '

He dragged her writhing body back over the fence, amazed at the strength of the girl who was almost a foot shorter than he was and would have weighed sixty or seventy pounds less. He was being forced to use all his strength.

'Nooooo,' she screamed again as she kicked herself upright, on his side of the fence now. Her right hand flailed through the air, fingernails slashing at his face.

He ducked, but not quickly enough. There was a burning, ripping sensation on his right cheek and he knew the flesh had been torn open.

'Bitch,' he yelled as she lunged at him again.

He parried her arm this time, blocking it with his forearm, and grabbed her throat with his right hand, using enough force to shock her but not to hurt her seriously. Then he swept his right leg behind hers, kicking away her feet. As she fell, he swung her right hand up behind her back.

'I don't know what you've done,' he gasped, 'but whatever it is ... Look, it's your arm that's going to get broken.'

His advice was wasted. She fought him all the way as he dragged her back along the High Street, trying to jerk away from him whenever she could and grabbing at his face and hair.

'Jesus,' he said softly when he saw the blazing house beyond the crowd of onlookers. The back wall seemed to have been blown out ...

(*A gas explosion?*)

... and bluish-yellow flames fringed in crimson darted out of the hole, spat from the windows and flickered in the depths of clouds of black curling smoke which poured from a long jagged rent in the roof.

A long line of men were passing buckets of water hand-to-hand, the last man throwing the water into the flames. McBaith knew that was a waste of time but reckoned the men knew that too. He guessed they felt that anything was better than just standing back and watching the house burn down without lifting a finger.

But where the hell was the fire brigade?

The girl began to thrash about even more violently as McBaith came up behind the crowd. He fastened a hand around the back of her neck and forced her to her knees, holding her there, trying to catch his breath.

Neil Ritchie appeared and took his arm.

'What's going on, Al?' he said, gesturing at the girl, his face taut with alarm. People had turned to stare at them now.

'You tell me,' McBaith said. 'I saw this girl running away from the fire. When I went after her she fought like a wildcat. D'you know her?'

'That's Fiona Andrews ... Ally Taggart's girl-friend.'

'What?' McBaith almost yelled the word.

'Did she do that to your face?'

'Yeah.'

Ritchie crouched down beside the girl then recoiled from her face which was a quivering mask of uncontrollable anger.

'Why did you run, Fiona?' he said. 'You didn't have anything to do with this, did you?'

She threw back her head and screamed frenziedly. 'I had tooooo. Let me goooo.'

Ritchie toppled off his haunches then leapt to his feet.

'In the name of God, what's wrong with her?'

'I was hoping somebody might be able to tell me.'

'I ... '

Ritchie was interrupted by a thick-set man with a black handlebar moustache.

'What's going on here?' the man said, glaring at McBaith. He looked at Fiona. 'Is she hurt?'

There was something about the man's tone that McBaith didn't like and he heard himself say: 'Who the hell are you?'

'Let that girl up.'
'I said who the hell are you?'
Ritchie raised his arms in a gesture of appeasement.
'Doctor Dunbar ... it appears Fiona started the fire.'
'What?'
'She's just admitted it. Mr McBaith saw her running away and caught her. Look ... see what she did to his face.'
'She's hysterical,' McBaith said irritatedly. 'I'd say the best thing would be to give her a sedative and get her to hospital.'
The doctor hesitated then said: 'Can you get her to my car? The ambulances haven't arrived yet.'
'OK.'
The doctor led the way along Gordon Street to his car and McBaith pushed Fiona into the back seat and held her while the doctor climbed in and opened his bag. The sight of the needle started a new outburst of shrieking and hoarse sobbing.
'Better make that strong, Doc,' McBaith said as the doctor filled the syringe.
He held the girl's arms while Doctor Dunbar inserted the injection but she fought him, thrashing her legs about and trying to butt her head into his face.
The sedative took effect almost immediately. McBaith felt the girl's strength ebbing away and, after a moment, she slumped into his arms.
'I don't understand any of this,' Dunbar said.
'That makes two of us,' McBaith said.
'I apologise if I was a little abrupt back there.'
'Forget it.'
'You're Malcolm's cousin, aren't you?'
'Uh-huh.'
'Well ... I'll get Fiona to hospital and we'll see what's what.'
'Will you have her checked for drugs?'
'Drugs.'
'Yes, drugs.'
'Of course, but I know Fiona and ... '

'Look, something is making her act this way.'
'I do know my job, Mr McBaith.'
'Sure, sure. I'm sorry.'

Neil and Janet Ritchie were waiting for him when he got out of the car.

'Oh good heavens, look at your face,' Janet said, reaching up and lightly touching the deep scratches on his cheek. Her eyes were filled with concern and that gave him a lift in a strange kind of way he couldn't describe.

'Didn't the doctor offer to patch you up?' she said, throwing an angry glance at Dunbar.

'I think he's got more important cases on his hands right now.'

She took his arm. 'I'll take you to my flat and see what I can do.'

Her arm remained linked with his as she led him along the back of the crowd and up the High Street.

Sirens wailed in the distance and she looked over her shoulder and said: 'Fire brigade at last ... or the ambulances.'

'Many people hurt?'

'The woman in the house got out all right ... but then the gas blew. I don't think there's anybody seriously injured. It blasted out the back of the house. Everyone was at the front. What happened with Fiona?'

He filled her in on the details of his chase and added: 'D'you still say there are no drugs in Aragarr?'

'I'm sure of it.'

He was going to argue but he swallowed his words. The hospital tests would provide the answer one way or the other.

They turned off the High Street into a narrow side street, went up a metal staircase on the outside of a building and entered a small cosy flat.

'Home,' she said, gesturing him to a large easy chair.

'It's nice,' he said, sitting down. The chair seemed to swallow him up, relaxing him instantly.

She disappeared into another room and returned a moment later with a bowl and some cotton wool.

'This'll sting,' she said, dabbing the cotton wool into the liquid in the bowl.

'I'll live,' he said.

She cleaned the wounds gently then dried his face and fetched some ointment which she smeared over the cuts.

'That should do it,' she said when she had finished. 'Like some coffee ... or something stronger?'

'Coffee? Yeah, that'd be nice.'

She strolled into the kitchen and he listened to her moving about there for a minute or so then stood up and walked to the door.

He stood watching her for a moment, leaning against the edge of the door. His mind was filled with questions about Taggart and Fiona and he had been going to put some of them to her but now he decided he would drop the subject for the moment.

'You know,' he said, 'I can't put my finger on it but you don't have the same accent as most of the people in Aragarr. It's different from the way your uncle speaks. I've got to admit British accents confuse me but ... '

'Neil Ritchie isn't really my uncle,' she said, pouring boiling water into two cups, 'and I'm not from Aragarr.'

'I guess that explains it,' he grinned.

'I hadn't actually met Neil until about a month ago when I came here to teach at the school – he helped me get the job. Neil is my father's cousin. I was born in Aberdeen but my family moved to London when I was ten. I was brought up there.'

'That's your life history. Maybe I should tell you mine.'

'I'm sure it'll be very interesting,' she said and flashed him a smile.

She left the coffee where it was, crossed the room and looked up into his face, standing close up to him. Their eyes carried on the same wordless conversation as before. She touched his unscarred left cheek softly, running her finger down it.

'You're very attractive,' she said.

'Yeah?'

'Yeah, but I'm sure you know that anyway.'

This is the strongest come-on I've had in years, he thought, then amended that. It was the strongest come-on he had ever had. She was giving him the come-on like *nobody* ever had before. He admitted to himself that he felt a little uncomfortable. He liked to make the moves himself.

'Well, don't you?'

'What?'

'Know you're attractive?'

'It's always nice to be told.'

He felt himself being drawn into her eyes, almost as if he was being hypnotised by them. Whatever it was this woman had she had a lot of it and he liked it.

She turned away and fetched the coffee and it was as if a spell had been broken. He walked back into the lounge ahead of her, took the coffee she handed to him and sat down in the big easy chair again.

She stood in the middle of the room sipping her coffee, not speaking, just watching him, and he was aware she was making him feel uncomfortable – for the second time.

Questions about the night's events began to nag at him and he broke the silence, saying: 'That old woman in the pub tonight ... what did she mean when she said too much has been happening and the answer wouldn't be found in the ... whatever it was she said?'

'In the world of men, that was what she said. I'd just forget it. Annie Stewart is a woman you can safely ignore.'

'She said it twice. Once when we were talking about Malcolm's nephew and then when I went to the bar to get some drinks. Has anything else happened ... besides what happened to the Taggart kid and Fiona?'

Janet sighed. 'Some tourists were killed ... up in the pine forest. They'd rented a chalet ... '

'Killed ... how?'

'Stoats.'

'What ... '

'Like weasels.'

'Oh, yeah. Isn't that kind of unusual?'

'Yes,' she said slowly. 'I've never heard of it happening before but ... who can tell with wild animals.'

'I guess you're right. Anything else?'

'Nothing important. Annie loves to be mysterious and to make a drama out of everything. She's a bit of a loony.'

He shrugged. 'There's a lot of them around,' he said.

They began to talk about everyday things – his search for his roots, what it was like being a teacher in Aragarr, his life in Los Angeles. He noticed for the first time that her face seemed to be filled with a kind of subtle movement, of fleeting, rapidly-changing expressions that were barely detectable. He had never seen a face that was so *alive*. She told him she was twenty-eight and single and he told her about Tina and the kids and said he was forty-one, resisting the temptation to knock off a couple of years. Half an hour slipped by.

When there was a lull in the conversation, he glanced at his watch.

'Guess I better get moving,' he said. 'Malcolm'll be wondering where in hell I am.'

'When will I see you again?'

'I'll be around Aragarr for a couple of weeks at least.'

'Call me whenever you like. Aragarr sixteen's the number.'

'OK, I'll do that.'

'I could show you around. Malcolm doesn't drive, you know.'

'No, I didn't know that.'

'You can borrow my car whenever you like.'

'That's friendly of you. Thanks.'

At the door, she rested her hands on his waist, stood on her tiptoes and kissed him softly, a brief brushing of their lips.

'I'm glad you came to Aragarr,' she said as he went down the stairs.

She was coming on strong and that was putting it mildly, he thought as he walked back to the hotel. Not that he minded. What troubled him a little was that he had found her so attractive so quickly. Not just sexually – something else as well. It wasn't liking or respect either – he didn't know her well enough for those things. Chemistry, he told himself at last, just chemistry pure and simple. It was corny but he could think of no better word.

It had been an eventful day to say the least, he thought, and Taggart and Fiona definitely presented a big puzzle. He had been a cop too long for it to be easy for him to just walk away from a puzzle.

Malcolm was waiting for him when he arrived back at the hotel, standing alone in the doorway, peering down the street like a worried mother.

'Are you all right?' he said as he led McBaith inside. 'I heard what happened with Fiona. How's your face?'

'It's all right. Janet Ritchie took care of it.'

Malcolm shook his head. 'I can't explain any of this,' he said.

'It beats me too,' McBaith conceded.

'Hardly the kind of welcome I'd wanted for you in Aragarr.'

McBaith nodded his agreement.

They sat down at a table in the main dining-room and talked for an hour, McBaith outlining the events of the evening, then Malcolm said: 'You must be worn out. Maybe it's time you went to your bed.'

McBaith stretched and said: 'Sounds like a good idea.'

He fell into a deep sleep the instant his head hit the pillow.

McBaith rolled over, blinked his eyes open and was instantly wide awake. For a moment he didn't know where he was. He searched for the familiar signs of home then his mind flicked through the events of the past week and he remembered.

Aragarr. McBaith's Private Hotel.

He wondered what had awakened him, listened for any sounds, any sign of movement inside the hotel or outside in the street, but there was nothing.

He closed his eyes and tried to go back to sleep but it was impossible – there was an alertness, a tension about him he couldn't shake off. He glanced at the luminous dial on his watch. Four-thirty.

He climbed out of bed, yawned and strolled to the window.

The harbour was placid, whispering against the sea-wall, and he listened dreamily to the muffled sound of boats clanking at their moorings for a moment before sweeping his eyes along the High Street, searching for the house which had been gutted by fire.

He found the Jacobite Arms but ...

... the house was between the pub and the far end of the High Street therefore his eyes must have gone over it without noticing it.

How was that possible, he thought drowsily, letting his eyes move back up the street.

There. There was the street, about forty feet from the pub – Gordon Street, it was called, wasn't it? – and yet ...

He couldn't find the house. On the corner of Gordon Street where the house should have been stood a circular stone tower. It was as big as a house at its base and seemed to taper to a smaller area at the top. He guessed it was about three storeys high, making it the biggest building in Aragarr ...

... yet he hadn't noticed it before. He hadn't seen it from the hilltop, or on his walk or when he chased Fiona or during the fire. And it was such a distinctive building. It looked like a museum or a historical monument.

He peered at it, his brow furrowing, and his eyes picked out a small window about halfway up the wall, level with his own. There appeared to be bars on the window and ...

Were those fingers wrapped around the bars?

Of course it had to be an illusion caused by distance and night and the weak light from the street lamps.

He leaned forward, staring.

Fingers. They *were* fingers. Old man's fingers formed into fists around the bars.

He narrowed his eyes and tried to look between the fists, into the cell, tried to see the man beyond.

Cell. Why had that word come to him? Why had he thought *cell?* This ancient tower couldn't be a prison ...

Then his eyes made out a face.

Two wide eyes. A nose ...

A putrid, rotten nose.

Flesh was hanging from the face in festering strips, the nose was a shapeless lump, the mouth was an ugly leprous hole and ...

The figure was beckoning to him now, one hand waving slowly through the air.

And the eyes seemed to be talking to him, communicating something to him ...

Something that he wanted to shut out, didn't want to hear, didn't want to know.

But what?

This is crazy.

Can't be real.

The words came to him like words on a distant neon sign coming suddenly into sharp focus.

It was crazy.

He had to drag his eyes away, go back to bed, but couldn't.

He tried to step away from the window but found he was held there by some indescribable force. A drowsiness washed over him but it wasn't like a sleep-drowsiness. It was ...

... like ...

Like he was being mesmerised, put into a trance.

Now it was as if all that existed in his entire world were the tiny window and the bars and that terrible face beyond.

And they were growing bigger.

(Bigger? Can't be. No ... can't be.)

YES. BIGGER.

He was gliding through the air, going towards the face.

He could make out details now that he hadn't been able to before. The eyes were bloodshot. There was a huge scar

on the forehead. There ...
    He gathered all the power of his will and ...
    (not happening, a dream, that's all)
    ... jerked his head away.
    He felt his legs beneath him, rubbery and weak.
    He was still in his room.
    (Of course he was. Where else could he be?)
He shoved himself away from the window, stumbled to the bed and fell into it. Sleep gnawed at him instantly, filling his brain with a misty drowsiness, dragging his eyelids closed like two heavy curtains. The bed seemed to embrace him, surround him with a cocoon of warmth.
    He was so tired now ...
    Exhausted.
    (But if he was that tired why had he woken up in the first place?)
The question stood alone in his brain for a moment, a solitary messenger in a dark landscape, patiently awaiting a reply. None came.
    McBaith began to slip away into sleep, compartment after compartment of his brain welcoming the oblivion, surrendering instantly.
    But there were other questions ...
    ... dim, jagged, formless things ...
He had to find some kind of explanation for what had happened, some anchor to hold him in place for the night, some answer no matter how unlikely.
    Illusion.
    Of course that was it. It had all been an illusion, the kind of thing that happens when the human mind is in that limbo between wakefulness and sleeping.
    Just an illusion.
    Nothing to get excited about.

Eight

Malcolm woke McBaith with a gentle shake of his shoulder.

'What ... oh, morning ... what time is it?' McBaith said.

He blinked at the sunlight which streamed in through the window and sat up.

Malcolm glanced at his watch. 'Ten past eleven,' he said.

'Sorry ... guess I've missed breakfast,' McBaith grinned.

'Nothing of the kind. No, as long as you're here you keep your own hours ... It's just that the police called to say they'd be here in about ten minutes to see you ... about Fiona.'

'OK. I guess they want a statement.'

He drew the bedclothes back and started to get up, but sat back when Malcolm spoke again.

'Fiona's dead,' he said.

'Dead.' There was a kind of sodden shock in the way McBaith spoke the word, as if he had just bitten into something soggy and rotten.

'Aye. She died in the early hours this morning.'

'What of?'

Malcolm shrugged. 'Maybe the police will tell you.'

'Yeah,' McBaith said slowly.

Malcolm left and he got up, shaved and dressed.

Dead. Fiona was dead.

He hoped Malcolm was right and the police did have some answers. He was going downstairs just as Malcolm was showing a man in a dark suit into the small smoking-room opposite the dining-room.

The two men paused on the threshhold and Malcolm said:

'Sergeant Smith, this is Al McBaith.'

Malcolm left them alone in the smoking-room and they sat down in two large easy chairs in front of a crackling fire.

'Malcolm tells me Fiona died,' McBaith said.

'Yes.'

'How?'

'We don't know. She went into a coma just after she arrived at hospital ... then her heart just seemed to give out.'

'Was she tested for drugs?'

'Yes, she wasn't on drugs.'

There was a brief, heavy pause, then McBaith said: 'Then what made her behave like she did?'

The policeman ignored the question and took out his notebook and a pen.

'If you could just outline everything that happened last night ... when you chased Fiona.'

McBaith ran through the events the policeman was interested in then signed the notebook where the policeman indicated.

'Did you use any undue force when you grappled with the girl?'

'No, I ... oh, now wait a minute?'

'Did you?'

'Not enough to kill her if that's what's on your mind,' McBaith said coldly.

'You're sure.'

'I'm sure.'

'I believe you were a policeman ... in America?'

'Yes ... which means I know how to grab someone so that they stay grabbed without having to seriously hurt them.'

'Of course.'

Smith flipped his notebook shut and tucked it into the inside pocket of his jacket.

'If she wasn't on drugs ... what theory are you working on?' McBaith said. 'Tell me ... off the records. I'm curious.'

'There hasn't been a post-mortem yet. When there is we'll be positive about the drugs angle. But we're sure enough now to abandon that possibility.'

'And?'

'This is not for public consumption.'

'I understand.'

'Did you know Fiona had psychiatric treatment?'

'No. I only got here yesterday.'

'Well she did. It's possible that what she did was a hysterical reaction to what happened to her boy-friend. She was very highly strung.'

'It's possible but isn't it kind of odd that both kids go off their nuts within a few days of each other?'

'From what I've heard the boy was very drunk. He was seen staggering about in the Jacobite Arms not long before the incidents which culminated in his death.'

'OK. Let's say it's not drugs. But don't the incidents look as if they're connected.'

'Yes. She had a hysterical reaction to the boy's death.'

'Couldn't there be ... '

He let the sentence trail away, his mind chasing possibilities, then jabbed a finger in the air and said: 'What about that stream back there ... could there be something in that, some kind of pollution?' As soon as he spoke, he knew he was grabbing at straws.

'Then why are there only two people involved?' the sergeant said with a hint of impatience.

'So far.'

'Why don't you just let us do our job, Mr McBaith.'

'Look, I don't want to butt in ... but I have a kind of personal interest ... ' He hooked his thumb over his shoulder ' ... living with Malcolm, you know.'

'Mr McBaith, drugs are not involved and there isn't anything in the Aragarr Burn.'

'I meant ... I don't know ... something ... from a factory or ... '

'The Aragarr Burn is as pure as anything you'll find anywhere in the world. There are no factories. It runs down from the hills.'

'Yeah, OK. D'you want me for anything else?'

'No ... Well, there is one thing I should mention. You're

not thinking of leaving the country in the near future are you? If you are, would you let us know.'

'OK.'

After the policeman left, McBaith found Malcolm in the kitchen.

'Well?' Malcolm said.

McBaith gestured helplessly.

'He didn't give me any real answers. Her heart just stopped. I don't get it.'

'But ... '

'The sergeant told me ... confidentially ... that they think she had some kind of hysterical reaction to Ally's death.'

He looked at Malcolm and saw that the older man's eyes were filled with a kind of pleading. It was as if they were saying 'You were a policeman, you come up with some answers ... ' They were begging for anything that would explain what had happened to Fiona and why his nephew had done what he did, anything that would make sense of it. It couldn't be easy for the old man, McBaith thought, living with the thought that his nephew had gone out of his mind on alcohol and gone on the rampage, killing and taking his own life.

But that was what had happened, wasn't it? The problem was that no relative ever accepted that their own kin could be guilty of terrible crimes. McBaith had seen it so often before.

'I don't have any answers,' he said to Malcolm. He was going to add: 'You just have to accept that the police theories about Ally and Fiona are probably right,' but he didn't – he swallowed the words.

They talked non-stop during lunch but the subject of Ally and Fiona was never mentioned – it was as if the men had decided to let the curtain fall on that subject for the moment.

But McBaith knew it hadn't gone far away – he could feel it burrowing away in his brain.

After lunch McBaith said he felt like a walk. Malcolm

couldn't come along because a painter was coming up from Wester Killich to give him a quote for the dining-room and the smoking-room.

It was as McBaith walked into his bedroom to get his coat that the sediment of the dream (or was it a dream?) from the night before began to gather together and form into a memory.

Yes ... what *had* he seen?

He walked to the window.

Was there really a Roundhouse?

He put both hands on the window sill then stood quite still, not looking out, just stroking his jaw and thinking.

Why had his mind conjured up the word *Roundhouse?*

Well, it was round wasn't it? It made sense to call it that. What else would he call it?

But the word had sprung into his mind as if he had known that was what it was really called – *the Roundhouse*.

It was a dream, for Christ sake, he told himself, and let his eyes travel along the High Street to Gordon Street.

Yes, just a *dream*.

There, on the corner of Gordon Street, was the fire-gutted two-storey house, the walls around the windows blackened by flames.

No sign of any old, round building.

No sign of any barred window with a strange figure beyond the bars.

He shrugged his shoulders into the coat and went downstairs.

'See you,' he said to Malcolm.

'Sorry I can't come.'

'That's OK.'

'Another day. We'll take a real walk, right up into the hills. By the way, we can take a trip along the coast in a boat one day if you like. I can easily arrange it.'

'Great.'

He stepped outside and a chill wind whipped at his coat. It had been raining but the sky was clear now, bright sunshine reflecting off the wet street.

He met Annie Stewart outside McCormack's shop.

'And how are you today, Mr McBaith, after all the excitement last night?'

'Afternoon,' McBaith said. 'I'm fine, just fine.'

'You'll have seen the police?'

'I've given my statement, yes.'

'Shame about Fiona.'

'Uh-huh. How are the other people who were hurt, have you heard?'

'Only two kept in hospital but they're not in any danger ... of dying I mean.'

'I'm glad to hear that.'

'And what are the police saying ... that Fiona was drunk too?' She gave a little cackle but there was no mirth in her eyes – it seemed to McBaith they were watchful and ... something else.

A little afraid? Was that it or was it just in his imagination?

'You'll have to ask the police about that,' McBaith said, 'but I guess they know their job.'

'Time will tell,' said Annie, 'but I'm thinking they'll be looking in all the wrong places.'

'Why?'

Annie thought a moment then said: 'Because they work in the narrow corridors laid down for them ... The answer to this lies beyond those narrow corridors. Well, goodbye Mr McBaith, perhaps I'll see you in the Jacobite Arms tonight.'

'Yeah, maybe. See you.'

Mysterious. The word lumbered into McBaith's mind. But wasn't it the word Janet had used the night before? Hadn't she said Annie Stewart was a loony who liked to be mysterious and make a drama out of everything?

McBaith intended his walk to last about half an hour but he lost track of time and walked most of the afternoon. It was one of those periods when thoughts just kept free-falling through his brain – about his past and his future, about

Aragarr and Malcolm, Annie Stewart and the fire, Ally Taggart and Fiona. And Janet.

He walked without having any positive idea of where he was going, up the steep hill to the main road – he considered going to his grandfather's cottage but the track was wet and muddy and he had light shoes on – then along the main road until he found a path that led into the pine forest. He stood for a moment looking down at Aragarr and the sea then turned up the path.

It began to drizzle and there was a kind of wet sighing as a sharp wind jostled through the pines. He was surrounded by a delicate, whispering patter-patter like the sound of muffled drums as the raindrops which ran down from the canopy of high branches fell to the carpet of pine needles.

The rain had stopped by the time he left the pine forest and headed back down the hill towards Aragarr.

He was deep in a daydream when the old woman appeared around a bend, shuffling towards him, taking minute steps.

'Hi,' he said but she didn't appear to hear him.

He could see she was very old. Her face was lined and seamed and wrinkled and there were bald patches in the dry, lifeless grey hair. She was wearing a black overcoat and black dress and he noticed that although both her shoes were black and had laces they were not of the same design.

'Hi,' he said again as she drew level with him.

This time she threw a suspicious glance in his direction and grumbled something before passing on.

As he reached the outskirts of the village he glanced at his watch and was surprised to find it was after four o'clock. Raising his head, his eyes picked out a sign on a newish-looking red-brick building – Aragarr Primary School, it read. His eyes swept left to the doorway and at that instant Janet Ritchie appeared.

And he had that weird feeling again – that feeling that he was trapped in his destiny, being led by the hand. It was as if he was meant to be here, meant to meet Janet, as if everything was unfolding as it had been planned.

He dumped the feeling, cast it aside like a piece of useless rubbish.

Dammit, it was ridiculous, wasn't it? His being there was pure chance. He could have come down the hill an hour earlier or an hour later.

He returned her smile and turned through the gate, meeting her in the middle of the schoolyard.

My God she was attractive, he thought. Even more attractive than he had realised the night before.

'Hi,' he said.

'Hello, Al. Nice of you to meet me.'

'I was ... uh ... just passing,' he said, almost apologetically.

She was carrying a huge pile of books and he took them from her.

'Thank you,' she said, then laughed: 'I was sixteen the last time a member of the opposite sex carried my schoolbooks.'

Again their mouths and their eyes were carrying on separate conversations.

'You've heard about Fiona?' she said.

'Yeah, this morning ... '

'I mean the post-mortem.'

'No.'

'I just saw Doctor Dunbar ... when he came to pick up his daughter from school. The post-mortem found nothing. No foreign substances. No explanation as to why she should have died ... or gone out of her mind like she did.'

'I know I've said it before ... but I don't get it.'

'I suppose the police will have a theory,' she said.

'Oh, they have.'

It began to rain and she said, 'That's my car' and pointed to a blue Ford.

He followed her to it and they got in.

'I've got to take some schoolwork out to a little boy who's been off sick,' she said. 'His parents are keen he doesn't fall behind. Why don't you come along for the ride?'

'OK.'

As they drove along, he told her what the police sergeant had said that morning, then added: 'It's a puzzle all right. Seems too much of a coincidence that something as weird as this can happen to two kids in the space of a few days.'

She shrugged and he added: 'I met Annie Stewart today. She was doing her woman-of-mystery act again. She's got me curious ... I just can't ever figure out what she's getting at.'

'Nobody can.'

'Look, I know about Ally and Fiona and you told me about the people who were killed by the stoats ... but you said other things had happened. What kind of things?'

She took one hand from the steering-wheel and waved it through the air in a brief dismissive gesture. 'Nothing important,' she said.

'You said something like that last night too,' he said, smiling curiously. 'It's almost as if you don't want to tell me.'

'No, it's not that,' she said quickly.

(*Too quickly?* he thought.)

'It's just ... ' She shrugged. 'Just that it's nonsense.'

He waited for her to continue and finally she did.

'A tourist went into the forest on the other side of the loch and he says he saw a stag in a clearing and it was ... well it was as if it was dancing, up on its hind legs.'

'Do they do that?'

'I've never heard of it. And there's more. He said it began to rush around the clearing as if it was chasing something then it began to hook its antlers about as if it was fighting another stag. I think he'd had too much of the water of life.'

'The what?'

'Whisky.'

'What else?'

'There was a woman up here from England visiting her cousin ... Mr McCormack. I don't know if you know him – he owns the shop.'

'We've never met.'

She braked and ducked her head, studying the road.

'Here's the farm,' she said, swinging the car along a muddy track towards a small cottage.

A dog barked from one of the outhouses, muffled, as if it was locked in. Janet drew the car to a halt. 'I'll be as quick as I can,' she said, reaching into the back seat and selecting two books from the pile he had set down there. The neck of her suit jacket fell open and he caught a fleeting glimpse of a white blouse, a blue and white necklace, the shoulder-strap of her bra and a slice of pale, soft breast-flesh. A tiny thrill ran through him, partly sexual, partly a sudden new awareness of her feminine vulnerability – an awareness that brought out a kind of protectiveness in him, what he would have ironically called his Sir Galahad instinct.

'Sure,' he said, looking away from her breast quickly. 'Take as long as you like. I'm in no hurry.'

As she walked to the cottage he found himself absently studying the fluid movement of her thighs through her tight skirt. Plump, he thought, slightly plump. But on her it looked good. He swung his eyes away when a woman in a blue dress and floral apron appeared at the cottage door.

While Janet was gone he flicked idly through the schoolbooks and watched black-faced sheep wandering about a sloping field strewn with boulders.

Then he heard her voice again. 'Goodbye Mrs Lothian. We all hope to see Colin again soon.'

She climbed into the car, smoothed her skirt down and said 'Sorry, if I took a long time.' He gave her his 'don't give it another thought' smile and they headed back towards Aragarr.

'You were telling me about McCormack's visitor from England,' he reminded her.

'Oh yes. Well she said she saw this man, an old man, in the pine forest. She said this man seemed to be coming after her. It scared her a lot and didn't sound like anyone from around here. She didn't get a clear look at the man but she said he was very old, had strange eyes and his face looked as if it was covered in sores. Like he was a leper or something like that, she said.'

Like the man in the Roundhouse, McBaith thought instantly, then jettisoned the thought irritatedly.

'She ran away from the man,' Janet continued, 'and fell and hurt her knee. Probably just some old fellow out for a Sunday drive who felt like a walk in the forest. I doubt if he really chased her.'

'When did this happen?'

'Last week.'

'And the incidents with the stoats and the stag?'

'All in the last couple of weeks.'

'And people don't think that kind of strange?'

'Oh, they do. That's the problem. Aragarr is very insular, the people are ... well a little old-fashioned, more than a little superstitious. That's why I don't like to talk about these incidents. I don't want things to get out of hand. There's no point in taking the case of a boy who gets too drunk and kills a man and a silly woman who gets scared in a forest and a drunken tourist and adding up two and two and getting five.'

And an American tourist who saw a Roundhouse that didn't exist and bars and a man with a rotting face, he thought.

(*Damn*. It had been a dream, that was all. And why did he always refer to it as *the Roundhouse?*)

'What are you trying to say,' he said.

'Just that some people are already talking about Aragarr hitting a bad-luck streak.'

'Hasn't it?'

'Yes, but when they say bad luck they don't mean what you mean. They think it's some kind of ... well, not curse exactly ... and not Biblical punishment ... but a bit like both. I know that doesn't make sense but I'm a newcomer here and it's hard to put into words. Their religion here is all hellfire and damnation. It's like ... if you get sick, it must be that God has a reason for punishing you. Not quite like that but something like that. I'm sorry I'm not explaining it very well.'

'I think I get the message.'

'Annie Stewart goes even further. She blames evil forces.'

'Yes, but she would. Your uncle doesn't pay much attention to her.'

'No, but he's worried too. Something is affecting the amount of milk his cows are giving and some of another farmer's cows died mysteriously.'

'Could there be something in the stream? I asked the police sergeant about that this morning and ... '

'No, it's not the burn. What could there be in the burn? There are no factories upstream, nothing like that. I'm sure all of this is just coincidence but others aren't.'

'But there's nobody else who believes in the evil eye ... things like that.'

'Not quite. But some of them are looking for answers ... and I don't like the places they're looking.'

'Where?'

'Let's just say halfway along the road Annie is on.'

'Yeah,' he said flatly.

'Of course you and I know that's silly. But I just hope nothing else happens. Let me put it this way. Some of the villagers are putting together all they believe has happened – half of which is sheer imagination, I'm sure of it – and trying to find an overall explanation.'

McBaith began to chuckle though he tried not to. 'What are you saying? You make it sound like they think it might be some kind of ancient Celtic earth god that's to blame and they're going to cut the throat of a lamb on some tall rock to appease him.'

'Not quite. But it's not something to make light of.'

He tried to look appropriately doleful and she laughed.

'Anything else happened?'

'Two other things. They both concern a woman who has just arrived in Aragarr. Meg Rees is her name. She makes jewellery. I bought this from her.' She lifted the silver-chained necklace from her chest and held it up for him to see. The medallion at the end was made up of a blue stone with white raised sections – two semicircles back to back.

'Very attractive,' he said. 'I met Meg Rees, up near my grandfather's cottage yesterday. She did seem kind of strange.'

'She's very nice actually. She's just ... different. But because she's new here, one or two people have mumbled something about her bringing the bad luck.'

'They can't mean that.'

'Just comments, that's all ... but it isn't very nice for Meg. I imagine if I didn't have relatives here they'd be saying the same about me. I'm a newcomer here too.'

'Maybe they'll blame me now,' he smiled. 'I could be next on the gossip hit-list. So tell me what happened to Meg Rees?'

'I'm not actually sure that anything happened. The sources for these stories aren't what I would call reliable.'

'Go on.'

'There's a character who's never out of the Jacobite Arms, Tommy Macleod is his name. He told Neil and anyone else who would listen one evening last week that he saw Meg sitting on some rocks below the loch road last week. He said he shouted to her but she didn't look up and when he looked closer she had an adder in her lap.'

'An adder?'

'Yes.'

'What do you think?'

'I think he'd probably had one too many.'

McBaith sniffed and said: 'What else? You said stories ... more than one.'

'The other one is so silly ... it's ... well, there's a boy at school ... He's not usually a storyteller but you can never tell and in this case I think he's telling a whopper. He's at that age, when fact, fantasy and growing up get people all mixed up. He said he saw Meg running through the woods at the other side of the loch ... and she was naked.'

He watched her and saw a tiny pink hint of a blush flood across the soft skin on the side of her neck and under her chin. He hadn't seen a woman blush in years and he found it tugging at some strings inside him, unwrapping parts of him that he had thought would stay wrapped up forever like forgotten parcels in a lost-property office.

'Naked,' he said slowly, almost as if he wanted to see if the blush would spread.

'Yes.'

'So she's a nudist. We've got those in California too.'

'This is not California. Anyway, it's probably a whopper of a fib ... boys of that age ... there's only one thing they think about.'

He was going to say 'What's that?' but he didn't, he said: 'Anything else?'

'Nothing worth mentioning. There's an old woman called Laurie Murdoch ... there are a few tales about her, and it's true she is strange. But she's just old, very old.'

'Does she wear black and have grey hair ... going bald?'

'That's her.'

'I saw her this afternoon. She had shoes on that didn't match.'

He swung his head around and saw that they had reached the bottom of the hill and were swinging past the school into the village. It had started to rain again, a fine drizzle matting the windscreen. She flicked at the dashboard and the wipers began to flip-flap.

'Will I see you at the Jacobite Arms tonight?' she said as she drew the car to a halt in front of McBaith's Private Hotel.

He tutted uncertainly. 'I'd like to but it's kind of up to Malcolm. I am his guest and I didn't see him at all last night. I'll try to talk him into coming.'

She pouted mock disappointment and he heard himself saying: 'Let's have dinner someplace tomorrow night. Is there anyplace around here?'

'There's a good seafood place at Wester Killich,' she said enthusiastically, her face beaming. 'I haven't tried it yet but I'd like to.'

'Sounds good to me.'

'If I don't see you tonight, I'll pick you up at about seven thirty.'

'OK.'

'Bye, Al.'

She used his name like nobody ever had before, letting it linger in her mouth. Her hand brushed his arm as he got out of the car, running from his shoulder to his elbow.

'See you,' he said, ducking through the rain. He waved from the doorway as she drove away.

Annie Stewart froze, the fork bearing a chunk of sausage three inches from her open mouth, as the strange electric shock sensation zipped through her. Slowly she put the fork back on the plate and looked around her kitchen. Of course there was nothing there ... but the sensation remained – a series of random *zings* like tiny electric currents darting through various parts of her body.

She knew instantly that the answers to all her questions about what had been happening in Aragarr lay in those tiny, slightly uncomfortable *zings* but couldn't explain how she knew. Her mind sprinted, but it was as if the answers were just out of reach, as if she was in a long corridor and the answers lay just around the next corner, tantalisingly close but still unreachable.

What was happening?

Then she realised the electric shock sensations were becoming hot, more uncomfortable, almost like flames licking over flesh and tendons, nerve ends and bones.

Many strange things had happened to her in her life but this ...

Something was trying to hurt her.

Alarmed, she stood up quickly, her eyes sweeping the room, blurring over a tiny porcelain man on the mantelpiece, a painting of a stag, a row of birch trees glimpsed through the window ... and coming to rest on the mirror.

Not her face.

But ...

Yes it was.

It looked like a slowly melting rubber mask, the features

dribbling into one another. Like a mask that had been left too close to a naked flame. The flesh of her forehead had run down her cheeks and white bone showed, her nose was a shapeless blob slowly sliding across her face and her mouth was folding into a long bleeding trench in her chin.

She was *burning*.

For an instant there was no pain, only blind terror. She was staring into her own eyes and they were disappearing into folds of ragged, shifting flesh.

Then the agony came, sudden as lightning. It was as if her face had been shoved violently into scorching flames.

She knocked over a chair as she ran into the hall, heading for the bathroom, instinctively seeking water to splash on the heat, panic clamping a fist around her throat.

Flames. The word seared through her mind. Like a message, a hint, a clue. But what did flames have to do with ...

She rushed into the bathroom, snatched on the tap and splashed cold water up into her face.

It made it worse.

The water felt like *acid*.

There was no escape from it.

She grabbed for the medicine cabinet. Cream might help and there must be ...

Her hand locked on the door and stayed there, not moving, not tugging the door open, as she caught sight of her face in the medicine-cabinet mirror.

There was no sliding flesh, no melting features now. Just her face, as it always had been. An instant later the pain disappeared, as if it had been snatched away.

A single bead of sweat edged out of her hairline and dribbled down across her cheek.

As she turned slowly away, she had the feeling that someone was laughing at her, had been playing some kind of trick on her. She couldn't explain that feeling but it lingered for a long time.

Nine

That night Malcolm told McBaith he still didn't feel like mixing with people. After they had eaten they sat in the two easy chairs facing the dining-room's bay windows, sipped whisky and talked.

The conversation began with the weather, switched to the history of Aragarr then moved to the incidents Janet had told McBaith about that afternoon.

McBaith noticed that the subject seemed to trouble Malcolm.

'What if Annie's right?' Malcolm said after a lull in the conversation, as if it was something which had been on his mind and which he had been trying to avoid discussing.

'Right?'

'Aye.'

'But ... '

'Annie has the gift, did Janet tell you that?'

'The gift?'

'The second sight ... sixth sense.'

'You mean she's psychic?'

'That's what I mean.'

McBaith didn't allow himself to smile.

'Do you believe?' Malcolm said.

'In what ... the paranormal, people who can see into the future, that kind of thing?'

'Yes.'

McBaith pursed his lips then said: 'No, I don't believe a word of it. I don't think any of what's happening in Aragarr has to do with ... evil forces.'

'Have you never seen anything to shake your convictions?'

'Never.'
'With Annie it isn't very strong. It comes and goes.'
'You mean she says it comes and goes.'
'Have it your own way.'
'You're not suggesting Ally's death has anything to do with ... what ... '
He waved his hands through the air as if trying to grab the right word.
'I don't know.'
McBaith found himself looking through the darkness beyond the window, at huge waves breaking over the sea wall.
After a moment, he said: 'You could set all the arguments side by side until they reached clear to China but you still wouldn't convince me. I think people just believe what it pleases them to believe. I was a Los Angeles cop for twenty years and I saw everything, every kind of loony and freak you can imagine. I came across churches run by crazies who believed Judas was the Messiah, communes where old men, little fat guys, seduced young girls by telling them that they were communicating with God or extra terrestrial intelligences through psychic tunnels. I arrested one creep who told me he could make office blocks fall down whenever he willed it. I think LA must have just about every kind of freak in the world and in all my years in the force I never saw anything with my own eyes that made me think it wasn't all just one big pile of junk.'
Malcolm studied McBaith's face for a moment then said: 'I'm not sure what to believe. I haven't seen anything with my own eyes either. I've always been considered a down-to-earth man, level-headed. I'm a good Christian and I believe in the power of prayer but ... beyond that I don't know ... '
'OK. I'll tell you what I will concede, Malcolm. I believe there may be powers in the mind we don't know about yet ... like maybe there are people who can bend spoons and nobody can explain why ... yet. But no more than that. I can't go for the evil-is-afoot-in-this-place kind of argument.'
'I know what you mean,' Malcolm said with a sigh. He

thought for a moment then added: 'We're in the late nineteen-eighties and even in such a remote place as Aragarr we really are quite enlightened. Nobody wants to listen to Annie but ... '

Malcolm paused when the wind rattled the window pane in front of them. McBaith thought he saw a quiver of fear move across his features.

Then Malcolm continued: 'There is something you don't know about,' he said with a sigh.

'What?'

'The night before Ally ... died ... I was in bed and I had this sudden feeling of ... I can't explain it properly ... I would say it was like danger. It was as if there was an intruder in the house but I knew it was not anything like that. I sat up and felt a kind of fear I've never known before. I did search the house but of course I found nothing. I had the feeling something was there ... and it was laughing at me. Then I looked at the lamp at my bedside and it was as if the light was not just a beam of light but lots of different pieces, small pieces. I prayed then ... kneeling beside my bed. It seems foolish to me, a man of my age being scared like that. But I was. In the morning I just put it down to the black mood that seems to have settled over Aragarr. It's like a grime that has gone into everybody and everything. For more than a week now I've noticed the strain. It's as if everyone wants to laugh their way through it but the laughter is strained, not very convincing, almost like that of people in an asylum.'

McBaith shifted his eyes away from Malcolm, deep in thought. That was when he saw the face in the window. It was his own reflection of course but he didn't realise that for an instant and it startled him, making his body tense up. Until that moment, he hadn't realised how jumpy he had become. The knowledge irritated him.

He found himself deliberately switching the conversation back to the real world, away from odd feelings and sensations. A black mood *was* gripping Aragarr. There was a kind of low-level collective hysteria. But the answer didn't lie there. He knew that. He was a man of the world and he knew the world was flesh and bone and rocks and asphalt and cars and highways.

They talked about McBaith's thoughts on drug abuse and possible chemicals in the burn, the kind of fertiliser the farmers might be using and even about the fall-out from Chernobyl but got nowhere.

It was when Malcolm came back after topping up their glasses that he said casually: 'If only Misty Isle wasn't so far away from the village, I'd think that might have had something to do with all this. You never know with places like that.'

'Misty Isle.'

McBaith took his whisky from Malcolm and put it down on the table in front of him.

'Yes. Misty Isle, the old chemical warfare place from the war.'

'You mean there's a place like that near here?'

'Aye.'

McBaith stared at Malcolm.

'Where?'

'Oh it's miles away, beyond the mouth of the loch, down the coast about a quarter of a mile. This can't have anything to do with that place.'

'Can't it.'

'It's been closed for more than forty years ... '

For the next half-hour McBaith pumped Malcolm for all the information he could get about Misty Isle – which wasn't much. During the war it had been the site of some kind of experimental station. At the time nobody in Aragarr had had any idea that it was more than a military base. There had been rumours – probably spread by the military – that it was a training station for commandos.

In 1946, when the base was closed, it had been mentioned in newspaper articles and books as a base where scientists had experimented on agents for the destruction of German crops.

'All the articles said the stuff they were working on was

harmless,' Malcolm said, 'but then they would, wouldn't they?'

The island could only be reached from the sea by someone in a very powerful boat who had an excellent knowledge of the reefs but it could be reached quite easily from the landward side. During the war the whole area had been sealed off but now, Malcolm said, anyone could row across the mouth of the loch and get to a point on the mainland opposite the island via a path through a birch forest. 'The path will be overgrown and it would be a good hike but it wouldn't be too hard,' the old man said. The island itself was only a true island at high tide. For most of the day it was accessible by simply walking over a beach.

When McBaith had finished asking questions, Malcolm said: 'Do you think … it could be … you know … '

McBaith shrugged, looking into Malcolm's eyes. They were desperate, ready to grab at straws. It would be more acceptable, more bearable, if Misty Isle or something like it was to blame, if Ally Taggart was the victim and not the perpetrator of crimes, McBaith knew. It would give some honour to his memory. McBaith could understand that.

'I suppose I could go out there and take a look around tomorrow,' he said slowly.

'I've got a little boat moored in the loch, you could take that.'

'OK. Yeah, OK.'

At least he could look. He owed Malcolm that much.

Liz Ballard had been the barmaid at the Jacobite Arms for more than ten years. She had first come to Aragarr on holidays, a Glasgow girl who wanted to see the countryside. An affair with an Aragarr fisherman had kept her there. The affair had finished when the man had come to realise that Liz was too much of a handful for him and had run away and joined the Royal Navy. Liz had just stayed on.

Plump and cheerful, Liz never let anything get her down. She had provided a lot of people with a shoulder to cry on in her decade in Aragarr and never had a bad word for anyone.

She had had a brief fling with Tom McNeil, the owner of the pub, but McNeil's wife had put a stop to that. Now forty had come to claim her and she guessed her marriage chances had become remote. It seemed strange to her that she of all people had never married. She had always liked men and knew that she would have made an excellent wife.

It was just fate, she told herself, and she wasn't one to dwell on misfortune. 'Don't worry about what you can't change, that's my motto,' she always said. There were always one or two tourists every year who took her fancy. Who knew? Maybe one day Mr Right would walk through the door.

It was eleven-forty-five and she had just managed to get rid of the last customer, giving him a friendly but firm shove out the front door. Now she busied herself washing the glasses, wiping down the bar, sweeping the floor and adding up the takings which she put in the upstairs safe before she left every night.

She had just opened the till when she first heard the scraping sound. It seemed to be coming from the wall behind her and she turned and studied it.

Then the noise stopped.

She was halfway through counting the cash when the sound came again, making her lose track of her total.

'Is somebody there?' she said, realising instantly that she had only said that because she was afraid, wanted to hear a human voice. It wasn't like her to be spooked by a sound, but so much had been happening in Aragarr lately.

The scraping stopped then started again before she could begin her count for the second time.

She stepped into the store-room behind the bar and flicked on the light. There was nothing unusual there, just boxes, barrels, bottles.

The scraping stopped but she carried out a thorough search. This was the only place the sound could have come from, unless it was outside.

Yes. Outside. That had to be it.

Probably a cat at the bin, searching for scraps.

Absently she tried to recollect the sound and analyse it as she counted the cash, piling the money on the bar in front of her.

Like a scratching, she thought, or like a saw.

No, not a saw. How could it be a saw? She smiled to herself.

A scratching or a scraping.

Or a gnawing ...

Like teeth chewing on old bones.

The words crept into her brain and she jumped, a tiny shiver trickling down her spine.

Teeth on old bones indeed.

How could she think such a thing?

She had just totalled the money and piled it into the cash bag when the sound started again, louder this time.

She flinched and tutted then tied the top of the bag and walked through the store-room to the back window. She drew it open and looked along the tunnel of light that spilled into the dim yard.

The sound was there all right, away to her left, along the wall.

A rough scraping, like paws or fingernails on stone.

'Anyone there?'

Why had she said that? Obviously it wasn't a person. It had to be an animal of some kind.

'Hey ... get away from there,' she yelled.

She heard a dull clunk-clunk, saw something roll over and lie still. It was a squarish shape but she couldn't make out what it was.

It was no animal, that was certain.

She stamped back to the bar, using anger to overcome fear, and carried the money up to the safe as the scraping continued.

When she had locked the money safely away and marched downstairs again, she slipped into her coat, glanced around the bar to make sure everything was as she wanted it and walked to the back door.

The rasping, scraping noise was louder than ever.

Then she heard the double clunk again.
Like stones ...
Or bricks?

She stood looking at the door handle for a long time, her hands on her hips. There was something out there and she had to find out what it was. What was she waiting for? What was she, some kind of a shrinking violet? She grunted a half-laugh. She had been called many things in her life but never that.

She took a deep breath, snatched open the door and stepped into the yard. There were dark patches (lots of dark patches) but there was plenty of light from the window and the door for her to make out all the familiar objects.

Scrape-clunk.

Away to her left. The same place as before.

The yard was invaded by silence now.

She marched over to the spot and bent over, peering into the dimness.

Bricks.

Five bricks were lying in an untidy heap.

Then she saw the hole in the wall, low down.

It was as if ...

... the bricks had just been *gouged out?*

They couldn't have been of course.

This couldn't be the source of the sound.

Not possible.

Who would creep up behind the Jacobite Arms in the middle of the night to rip bricks out of the wall?

No, they had probably been out for a while. Tom McNeil probably knew all about them. How long was it since she had been in the yard? Months. She would mention the matter to him the next day, but she was sure there would be a straightforward explanation.

A cat or a dog had probably wandered into the yard and bumped the bricks. Yes, that would be it. That made sense.

She walked back to the door with the strange feeling that eyes were boring into her back.

Imagination.

As she stepped inside she was aware that the yard was filling with a terrible stench, a rotten dead-flesh odour.

She didn't look back.

Imagination again. *Wasn't it?*

Had to be.

Had to be.

As she locked up she tried to pretend her hands weren't shaking, tried to ignore the fear signals her brain was sending out.

She hurried home, walking so quickly, she stumbled twice in her three-inch heels.

She didn't relax until her front door was securely locked and bolted behind her and even then a strange apprehension lingered.

Ten

As he rowed across the mouth of Loch Aragarr in Malcolm's boat the next day, Al McBaith was glad he had kept in condition over the years. The loch narrowed at the mouth to no more than two hundred and fifty yards and the water was smooth yet by the time he neared the far bank his arms and shoulders ached. There was a broad shaft of pain from the middle of his back to the base of his spine and a score of other muscles he couldn't put a name to tingled and quivered. He guessed it would have been easier if he had spent more time on the rowing machine in the gym and less time with heavy weights and on the track.

He dragged the boat up onto the beach where Malcolm had told him to – just east of the rocky outcrop – and found the path a few minutes later, running south through the birch trees.

The path wasn't as overgrown as Malcolm had warned him it might be and walking was quite pleasant. It was cold but the trees sheltered him from the wind and the sun appeared from time to time, peeping through the canopy of dark grey clouds.

He found the island easily enough. The path swung down to a beach then forked back into the trees again. Beyond the beach was the island – a small pyramid of grey rock and tussocky green grass. As he strolled across the beach he saw the scars man had left on the island from the time they had used it for the grimmest of purposes: Two Nissen huts on a grassy shelf near the top, what looked like the remains of a prefabricated house – but without the roof – a wooden fence which had toppled over and a long mesh fence brown with rust and topped by barbed wire.

The pools of water on the beach soaked his feet and the long grass on the island's steep eastern face drenched his trousers to the knees. By the time he reached the buildings his shoes were squelching and the wind was flapping his trousers, heavy with water, against calves numbed by cold.

He didn't know what he was looking for, therefore it was difficult to know where to start. The first Nissen hut was bare and wet, with puddles on the rotting wooden floorboards. The second contained a single filing cabinet with two editions of a wartime newspaper. The prefabricated building was as bare as the first Nissen hut.

Nothing.

He grinned wryly to himself as he walked about the compound around the buildings. You had to laugh. He had rowed across a loch, walked through a forest and got soaking wet – for what?

And what had he expected? A secret document about nerve gas signed by Winston Churchill and stamped top secret? Yeah, you had to laugh all right.

Yet something wasn't right in Aragarr and the answer could lie here even if he had to dig a little to find it.

Dig.

The word stuck in his mind. Could something have been sealed in containers and buried in the rocks? It had been done before. Wasn't granite supposed to be one of the best places to seal even such toxic material as nuclear waste? He climbed among the crags but found no obvious abnormality in the rock face. He knew there was little point in searching the grass area because any trenches would have been overgrown by now, but he did a quick check for any abnormal mounds – and failed to find anything.

He decided it was digging of another kind that was needed. Digging for information. There had to be some kind of expert he could call who would be able to tell him just what kind of experiments had been carried out on Misty Isle during the war.

What was happening in Aragarr *had* to be tied into drugs or chemicals, he reasoned, and wasn't it too much of a coincidence that a place like this base was so close?

Not right.

The words jumped into his brain.

Why?

He thought about them as he climbed back down to the beach.

Not right.

What else then? There had to be a rational explanation somewhere. Didn't there?

He crossed the beach, not bothering to avoid any of the puddles now, and started back along the path.

He decided he would ring a couple of universities, get the name of an expert on chemical warfare who could tell him what he wanted to know or get onto a library in one of the bigger cities and ask them what they had on Misty Isle – but he would get to the bottom of it one way or another.

Not right.

Why did those words keep ringing in his mind like a bell tolling slowly?

Halfway back to the boat he reached a point where the path hooked along a shoulder of land that fell away to a small beach, a ten-feet wide, fifty-feet long parcel of sand.

And that was when he saw Meg Rees for the second time.

She was naked ...

(in this cold!)

... and standing at the water's edge, facing out to sea, her fair hair whipping up behind her, baring her shoulders. The weight of her body was leaning on one leg rather like a child might stand. One hand dangled at her side and the other appeared to be held up to her face, as if she was idly sucking the tip of one of her fingers.

He did a double-take, walked on a few paces, then hesitated.

Should he talk to her? Would she be embarrassed?

He took a few more steps, heading for the point where the path disappeared back into the forest, still watching her, undecided about what to do.

Then she seemed to sense he was there.

She turned slowly and he stopped and faced her.
'Hello,' she said.
'Hi. Look, I'm sorry. I always seem to be butting in on you in your private moments.'
'I don't mind.'
She seemed totally unconscious of her nakedness, not in a brazen way but in a way that was without guilt. Her hair danced around her face, her eyes held his like a child's and her smile was open and friendly. Her expression and demeanour were just the same as if she had met him with all her clothes on in Aragarr High Street.
'How are you liking Aragarr?' she said.
'Oh ... it's great, yeah.'
He hunched his shoulders down into his overcoat, shielding himself from the wind. If he was so cold how was she able to stand there like that?
'How's the jewellery business?' he said.
'Oh, fine.'
'I met Janet Ritchie ... she's got one of your necklaces.'
'Yes.'
'It was very attractive. Hey, aren't you cold down there?'
'Not very. That's all in the mind. I was just going for a swim.'
He looked beyond her, at the sea. It looked grey and cold and about as uninviting as any sea could look.
'Out there?' he said.
'Yes, I swim every day. Why don't you join me?'
He laughed huskily. He had nothing against alternative lifestyles, he told himself, but this girl just had to be crazy.
'No, I don't think so, not today,' he said. 'You go ahead. I'm heading back. I'm getting cold just standing here.'
'Bye.'
She waved (like a kid waving at a school bus, he thought) then spun away and began to run into the water. It was a beautiful sight. When God had made women, McBaith thought, He had picked all the right parts and got them in all the right places. There wasn't much doubt about that. Her back fell in an exquisite triangle from shoulders to

narrow waist and the muscles of the buttocks and legs moved with the rhythm of running as first her ankles then her knees kicked through the waves.

Suddenly his eyes began to mist over and he felt like he was going to fall down. He thrust out his right leg and steadied himself, his eyes clearing again. He stared at the girl and it was as if she was moving in slow motion now, her legs kicking up great streams of water. But the water was not connected now – it was fragmented, divided into tiny chunks of light.

Like pieces of shining glass.

Or diamonds.

Hadn't Malcolm said something about the light in his bedroom appearing to fragment into separate particles?

Hadn't he?

McBaith didn't want to turn away. He felt like he wanted to stand there forever, just watching the girl. It was like he was being hypnotised.

It required all his will to turn first his head then his body away and start along the path.

He heard a splash as he entered the forest and looked back once. Her head was bobbing about in the water, her arm raised in a wave.

Something in the air. There was something in the air in Aragarr. Something ...

Misty Isle. It had to be and ...

Not right.

The words tolled in his head again.

Not right.

Not Misty Isle.

The thoughts dropped from his brain as the atmosphere about him seemed to change. It was as if the air in the forest had grown heavier, become compressed, as if it was being crushed in around him.

Just like at his grandfather's cottage.

Like the atmosphere before a storm. But more than that, more exaggerated.

And the fear he had known for the past month returned too. A nameless fear with no source he could identify.

He began to move more quickly, his feet rushing across the ground just short of a run.

Why? What ...

It was crazy, wasn't it?

Something in the air ...

Misty Isle?

Not right.

Then he heard something coming towards him through the forest, moving fast, brushing branches, ploughing through grass and fallen leaves.

The fast walk became a run as he looked over his shoulder and caught a glimpse of a face among the trees.

An old man's face.

No, not old. *Dead*. A dead man's face. The flesh hanging hideously, the nose putrid.

Yet not dead. There were eyes which were very alive, bloodshot eyes that watched him with a fixed, somehow amused stare.

And a scar on the forehead.

Scar?

The word burned its way into his brain.

It was the man from the Roundhouse. The man he had seen in his dream.

He stumbled on a patch of tussocky grass and almost fell but managed to right himself and run on, sprinting between the jagged lines of trees, his breath coming in short gasps, his heart hammering.

He threw a glance over his shoulder but couldn't see the man. What he did see was the bushes away to his right shaking and trembling as if giving way to something passing through them.

The man was moving parallel to him, he thought. Trying to get past him. Going to come out on the path up ahead of him.

He kicked harder, his feet bounding across the uneven ground, cold unreasoning fear clutching at the back of his neck.

The trees seemed to be closing in on him now, drawing

together as if they meant to block the path. Branches whipped at his clothes and snatched at his face. Surely the trees hadn't been this close together when he had been going the other way?

Of course they were, a voice in his head told him. Trees were rooted in the ground. Forests didn't move.

Birnam wood do come to Dunsinane, a crazy voice in his head shrieked. Christ, his brain was quoting Shakespeare at him now. Now of all times.

Keep your imagination under control, he told himself. The forest is just what it was before. Unchanged, not threatening. And why the hell are you running away from an old man anyway?

But the thought didn't entice him into slackening his pace, didn't ease the cold terror which pumped through him.

He glanced over his shoulder again and this time he saw the man. About twenty yards away to his right. Heading straight for him now. McBaith's eyes didn't linger on the man but in the instant they locked with that face and the stunted figure beneath it he had the impression the man was moving fast ...

But not running.

Travelling too smoothly for running.

Drifting.

Gliding.

McBaith heard a sound escape from his lips. It had no name. It was not a sigh or a scream or a yell. It was like the distilled essence of terror, a breathed whisper as quiet as a knife slicing meat.

His shoulder thudded into a tree, wrenching his collarbone, scraping flesh from his arm. But he felt no pain.

As he ran into a bend in the track, he saw the path widen up ahead ...

Broadening as it approached the loch?

He seemed to recollect the path had been wider there.

Or was that just wishful thinking?

Was it ...

Then he saw the loch with its green banks and the rocky outcrop and Malcolm's boat and an immense relief surged through him, like a fist releasing its grip on his heart.

A chance?

Maybe he could escape.

(*Escape what?*)

(He didn't seek an answer.)

Five galloping strides took him to the boat and he dragged it frantically into the water, gave it a shove and jumped in.

He was facing the way he had come when he grabbed for the oars and his eyes searched the forest for any sign of the man.

But there was nothing.

Nothing.

Just trees moving in the wind, hunched bushes and bobbing grass.

He rowed, violently gouging the oars through the water, thrusting aside the absurd thought that a hand was about to break the surface and grab for him. He settled into a steady rhythm and as he reached the centre of the loch the terror began to diminish, drawing back into a small corner of his brain.

He started to try to rationalise what had happened and laughed once to himself, but it was a nervous, uncertain laugh. Had it just been his imagination? Had there really been an old man in the forest? If there had been so what? It wasn't the man from his dream. It couldn't be. He was being caught up in Aragarr's collective hysteria. Cynical, worldly, street-wise he might be ... but he had been scared back there ...

... as those trees had closed in.

(Hadn't closed in. *Imagination.*)

(No old man. Just a mind trick.)

Of course there was something here that wasn't right. Something about Misty Isle or something he hadn't stumbled on yet but he'd find the answer and then ...

No.
The word hung in his brain with a terrible certainty that he couldn't dismiss.
Not right.
Not Misty Isle. Nothing like it. Something else.
(But *what?*)
He tied up Malcolm's boat at the small wooden pier on the northern bank of the loch and strode back towards the village.
What was the procedure if there were no answers, he asked himself and the reply came instantly. You took the facts and investigated them until the answers came. That was how it was done. There was no other way.
By the time he was approaching the village he had managed to jettison most of his fear, clear his mind, dismiss the thoughts he considered useless.
It was as he walked around the last twist in the road and entered the village that he saw the old woman.
He put her at about seventy. She was seated on a stool in front of a wooden hut, her fingers working quickly in the folds of a net. Her dress was long and black and she was wearing an old shawl full of holes. Grey hair peeped from beneath a black woollen hat.
His stride faltered as she looked up, her face twisting into a toothless grimace.
She just didn't seem to ...
To *what?* he thought.
To *belong*. To be *right* in this place.
(In this century?)
She ...
He managed to mutter 'Hello' but she didn't reply, just stared at him.
Why hadn't he seen that wooden shed when he had walked this way before? It was so interesting, so old. There was no glass in the windows, he noticed. They were covered by black wooden shutters of a kind he had never seen before. And ...
He shifted his gaze to the High Street.

But it wasn't the High Street.
Wasn't Aragarr.
The main street wasn't even sealed. It was just hardened mud.
And the houses were a mixture of stone cottages and wooden shacks with grey smoke dribbling from ancient chimneys.
He must have taken a wrong turning, he decided, must be in the wrong village.
Then he saw the huge rocky promontory Aragarr people called The Rock and his eyes flicked to the harbour.
There were about thirty boats tied up there, low, black crafts with tall masts.
Masts.
He walked on automatically, his brain searching for answers that didn't exist.
He saw that there was no sea wall, but the reef was there, just beyond where the sea wall should have been.
Not Aragarr.
Couldn't be.
He passed a group of people, trying not to look at them. They had been working on a huge net but had stopped now in various postures to stare at him as if he had two heads. They were dressed oddly, sturdy women in full, dark dresses and strange-looking shawls and heavily-bearded men in thick, broad-belted black trousers and woollen pullovers. Two of the men were wearing jackets...
Jackets that belonged in a museum.
Appear natural, a voice in his head told him.
What did that mean?
Where was he? What was happening?
Maybe he had never walked this far down the High Street before? Maybe this was the old part of Aragarr?
But the boats? The sea wall? The unsealed High Street? His eyes swept the street ahead of him, searching for something familiar – the Jacobite Arms or Malcolm's hotel or ...
And that was when he saw the Roundhouse.
Something that felt like acid ran down inside his spine,

burning everything away. When it had finished, the empty spinal column was filled with crushed ice.

He drew level with the Roundhouse and his eyes picked out a heavy wooden door reinforced with metal and a barred ground-floor window.

He tried to hurry past, dragging his eyes away from the building but he felt his pace slowing, his eyes being dragged remorselessly back ...

And up.

His head tilted back until he was looking directly at the second-storey window he had seen in his dream.

There were the bars.

There were the fingers.

The rotten face beyond grinned at him, bloodshot eyes staring.

He knew he had stopped walking, knew he was standing quite still.

But now it seemed as if there was nothing in the world except those bloodshot eyes.

And he felt the same drowsiness he had felt in his dream.

(But it hadn't been a dream, had it? *No*. And this was no dream.)

Suddenly it was as if he was weightless, was rising off the ground.

Then he was level with the face, looking into those eyes, staring at the bloodshot-red veins which streamed away from the dark brown pupils.

Icy-cold barbs of terror exploded through him, numbing his brain, chilling his flesh.

He tried to jerk his head away, thrashing it about until his shoulders ached, but there seemed to be no escape.

He wanted to look anywhere but into those eyes. He snatched his eyes up to the long, ugly scar on the forehead, down to the putrid, rotting nose, sideways to the grey stone wall beside the window.

Anywhere.

Anywhere but into those eyes.

The man seemed to be talking to him but there were no

words and his lips did not move. He seemed to be communicating something that McBaith did not want to hear, wanted to shut out at all costs.

Something told him that if he listened to the man, his life would never be as it had been before.

McBaith felt his head being drawn around as if by invisible hands. No escape. No way to avoid those eyes. He closed his eyes tightly but they sprang open again.

He was looking directly into the pupils now and he could see ...

No. He would *not* see.

He jerked his face away, looking past the man into the filthy, dark cell beyond.

And he saw that the man was not alone.

There were two other people in the dimness beyond.

Two naked women.

They were cavorting in one corner of the cell, laughing shrilly and fighting in a light-hearted way over some kind of a goblet.

'He has come,' the man seemed to say but there were no real words. Instantly, the women stopped struggling, one lying on top of the other. The one on the bottom turned towards McBaith and shook her hair from her face.

It was Meg Rees.

'So you've come,' the woman said. It was Meg's voice but the words did not seem to come from her.

'Yes, my Meggy, he's here to fulfil his destiny.' Words without speech, communication without sound. 'The Day of the Five is near.'

Then the man half-turned to the women and instantly McBaith felt the muscles of his legs tightening, his feet touching ground.

He was walking, hurrying along the earthen street, aware that eyes were watching him from the windows and doorways of cottages, the memory of those bloodshot eyes branded on his brain.

He would run, get out of the village, get to the main road, hail a bus.

Then he saw Malcolm's hotel, just as it had been when he left. Nothing in Aragarr was the same ...

Except that.

But what about inside?

He threw the door open.

Nothing had changed inside the hotel.

What was happening?

'Malcolm,' a voice shouted, hoarse, afraid, like the plaintive last words of a condemned man. It was his voice.

There was no answer.

'Malcolm.'

He was level with the desk now and his desperate eyes saw the note.

He snatched it from under the telephone on the desk and scanned the two lines of scribbled writing.

'Al,' it read, 'If you get back before I do, I'm away to do some shopping. Back in an hour. Malcolm.'

He put the note down, flopped into the chair behind the desk and buried his face in his hands.

Explanation! There had to be an explanation for all this. It had nothing to do with the other things that were happening in Aragarr of course. How could it? No it was a mind trick. The kind of thing that usually happened to old people who imagined they were back in their youth or crazy people who thought they were Napoleon or people under severe stress who thought they were back in a war that had ended ten years before. His mind had slipped a cog or two, that was all. Nothing else.

But maybe it *was* connected with everything that had been happening. He was hallucinating. Hadn't Fiona been hallucinating?

Misty Isle.

He had to follow up on that.

Had to do something that was real, something that made sense.

His eyes fell to the telephone and he snatched up the receiver. Flicking open the telephone book he found the operator's number and dialled.

A voice said 'Which town please?'
Town? A big city. Any one would do.
'Edinburgh,' he heard himself say. 'I'd like the number for Edinburgh University.'
She gave him the number and he flicked at the receiver and began to dial again.
Not right.
Not Misty Isle.
Not drugs, not chemicals, nothing like that.
Something to do with Aragarr's past? A small voice asked the question.
Why had he been whistling an old Aragarr tune when he had arrived in the village? How had it come to him? Why had he had that constant sense of fear? Why had he had the weird feeling of destiny? What was the meaning of the numbers which kept jumping into his mind? Why had he seen the Roundhouse and that man? (And why did he call it the Roundhouse?)
Of course everything was connected.
Yet he had to make the phone call, had to grab for the rational.
If it wasn't drugs or chemicals or nuclear fall-out or some other damned thing like that, what was it?
He spoke to five people at the university over a period of fifteen minutes and normality began to seep back into his veins. He discovered there had been quite a lot of bacteriological experimentation in Scotland and dumping of chemical weapons off the coast. The last person he spoke to gave him the name and phone number of an author who had written a highly respected work on chemical and bacteriological weapons.
He hung up, took a pad and pen from the desk drawer and dialled the author's number. The man was very helpful and more than willing to talk at length about German nerve gas and mustard gas being dumped at sea after the war, experiments in which animals were lowered from Royal Navy ships onto rafts, sprayed with clouds of germs, then taken ashore to be examined, and bacteriological

experiments at various sites.

And Misty Isle?

The author used various long names for the bacteriological weapons which were tested there then added: 'None of these things could have any affect on man. Even if they could they were never kept on Misty Isle in any quantity – just enough for lab experiments. The station opened late in the war and never had time to develop into a major base. The material tested was all bacteriological, no nerve gas, nothing like that, anti-crop agents, that's all. Certainly nothing that could have the effects you've described.'

McBaith thanked the man and hung up. That seemed to settle the matter. There was nothing on Misty Isle that could be making people hallucinate.

Therefore ...

Therefore what? he asked himself.

You won't find the answer in the world of men. The words jumped into his head. Wasn't that what Annie Stewart had said?

What was the alternative?

Three people were dead. Was he in danger? Was Malcolm? Was Janet?

He sighed and forced himself to stand up and walk towards the dining-room window. What would he see? The Roundhouse? Dirt streets? Old ships with masts?

What did it mean?

His heart began to beat faster as he raised his eyes to look along the High Street.

Tarred streets. The Jacobite Arms. Modern boats in the harbour. The sea wall. The burned-out shell of the house which Fiona had set on fire.

Everything was as it had been when he had first walked down the hill into Aragarr.

Then he saw William Macpherson, the garage owner, and the big man waved and smiled. McBaith opened the window and they talked, just passing the time of day.

When Macpherson left, McBaith lowered his head until his forehead touched the cold window pane and stood staring down at the earth for a long time. There had been times before when things hadn't made sense to him – when people killed for no reason, when old women were stabbed for their shopping money, mindless vandalism, villages wiped out in pointless wars, bombs in airport terminals. But all of these things were part of the human condition.

What was this?

When Malcolm returned, McBaith led him into the smoking-room and told him everything.

Malcolm didn't say a word while McBaith was speaking but his eyes spoke, showing despair, defeat and a thin fear.

'It's not Misty Isle then?' he said when McBaith was finished.

'No,' McBaith said then added: 'Malcolm, I have to know what's happening to me, to this place. What did I see in that street out there?'

'I don't know, I just ... '

'It wasn't just a hallucination, was it?'

'I ... '

'Malcolm, I feel like we're all in danger. That building I mentioned, the round one with the barred windows ... where I saw the man ... was there ever a building like that in Aragarr?'

Malcolm nodded slowly, reluctantly. 'Aye, there was.'

'When?'

'Not in my lifetime! A long time ago. I saw a drawing of it when I was at school ... it was up on the wall in the old schoolhouse.'

'What was the building called?'

He had deliberately not used the word Roundhouse when he was outlining the events of the day to Malcolm and now he studied Malcolm like a man watching a judge, awaiting sentence.

'It was called the Roundhouse,' Malcolm said and McBaith's heart jumped.

(Not drugs. Not chemicals. Not Misty Isle. You'll not find the answer in the world of men. *Jeeesus*, what was going on?)

'What was it used for?' McBaith said.

'It was knocked down at about the turn of the century. At that time it was a kind of general storehouse. Before that it was ... like the local jail.'

McBaith sat in silence for a long time then got himself a whisky.

When he came back, Malcolm said: 'Did you hear about the Jacobite Arms?'

'What about it?'

'Half of the back wall collapsed during the night.'

Eleven

'I don't believe it,' Janet said incredulously when McBaith finished speaking, taking her eyes off the road for an instant to glance at him. They were driving south, heading for the sea-food restaurant in Wester Killich and he had talked non-stop for fifteen minutes, pouring out everything to her.

It wasn't her words that made him pause, it was the way she said them.

'What do you mean?' he demanded.

'I mean I find it hard to believe that you of all people are getting caught up in the ... hysteria in Aragarr. Maybe hysteria is too strong a word but you know what I mean.'

'I ... '

'So a hotel wall fell down. It was an old building. Have you ever heard of subsidence? You were whistling an Aragarr tune. Maybe you heard it on the bus or on the radio, maybe your grandfather whistled it to you when you were a little boy. Who knows? You and Malcolm have both had a strange feeling of fear. So what? I had one of those last week and the week before that and a month before that ... I've had them all my life. I thought everybody did.'

'Not like this, I ... '

She put her hand on his thigh. 'Al, think about what you're saying. A hotel wall falling down is somehow tied in to arson and murder?'

Suddenly he felt foolish. 'I know what I saw today.'

'An old man in the forest?'

'Not just an old man?'

'No ... you saw Meg as well. I think you must be a Peeping Tom. If you'd had any decency you would have given poor Meg a big berth and avoided embarrassing her.'

She squeezed his leg to tell him she was only joking.

'It was so damned cold out there.'

'I've heard of lots of people who swim in all weathers. Isn't there a club somewhere they call the Sub Zero Club. They swim every day no matter what the weather. I don't think they actually swim among icebergs but close to it.'

'OK, OK. What about what I saw in the village?'

'You mean that's linked to Fiona and Ally? To murder and arson? Aren't you just doing what Annie Stewart and some others are doing? Adding two and two and getting five. How could what you saw have anything to do with a drunken boy killing someone and a hysterical girl? How could it have anything to do with tourists being killed by stoats?'

'Stoats don't usually kill people, do they?'

'With wild animals, who knows what they'll do. Family pets sometimes kill their owners.'

'Explain it then. Explain what happened in the village.'

'These things happen. They're rare, Al, but they happen. I've read about it. Everything that's ever existed leaves a trace of some kind ... I can't explain it really ... people and things leave behind a kind of an aura and occasionally people see things that don't really belong in the time they're living in. It just happens. Fifty years from now when we're all living in the huge glass domes that science-fiction writers love so much we'll know why.'

'So how come I saw Meg Rees ... in the Roundhouse?'

'Maybe you fancy her. Who knows. It was your hallucination.'

He began to laugh despite himself and she joined him.

'I'm a little jealous,' she giggled. 'If you have to hallucinate, hallucinate about me.'

He threw his head back, roaring with laughter.

When she spoke again, she imitated an Aragarr accent.

'There's some that will believe anything,' she said, 'no matter what kind of foolishness.'

The memories of the day were suddenly distant, removed to a corner of his brain.

'Laughter is a good cure,' she said.
'Yeah.'

He dropped the subject then and they began to talk about other things — swapping jokes, telling funny stories about things that had happened to them, exchanging philosophies, talking about their lives. He found she had a soothing effect on him. He could feel the tension that had knitted its way into the muscles of his shoulders slipping away.

A few minutes later they drew into Wester Killich, which was about twice the size of Aragarr. 'A metropolis,' he observed with a grin.

'But not as friendly as Aragarr, not as nice,' she said. 'It's got three restaurants though. Do you like seafood?'

'Love it.'

'That's something else we have in common.'

The Bay Restaurant was small — five tables with a seating capacity for twenty — and was run by an elderly couple who took McBaith and Janet for a married couple. They didn't bother to correct the error.

The food was delicious. She had baked trout, he had lobster with avocado and they shared a bottle of Riesling.

They talked and laughed throughout the meal as if they had known each other all their lives and when they had finished, just as Janet was pouring the last of the wine into his glass, a thought flashed into his mind. It came with such suddenness that she commented on his strange expression — but he managed to explain it away with a joke.

The thought was a simple one but it caught him unawares, threw him off balance, confused him.

He was falling in love.

He hadn't thought of himself as the falling in love kind. Not at his age. Love was the kind of word teenagers used ('Do you love me?' — 'Oh yes, I love you so much.' Smooch-smooch.) It didn't seem to fit with him. He had never thought he would feel this way about a woman again, had forgotten it existed. He had felt that way about Tina so many years before — but he had only been in his twenties then. By the time he had reached his thirties – and he and Tina had been married for seven years – he had stopped using the word, left it behind with his youth. Since Tina's departure, there had been a lot of women – some were friends, some were bed partners, some were both. He had been very fond of a couple of them but there had never been any ...

He found himself searching for the right word, settling on it just as the woman who had served them brought the bill.

Magic.

Yes, that was the word.

Magic.

It was as they left the restaurant, planning to head for a pub which Janet had heard was pleasant and quiet, that she slipped her arm into his and breathed: 'Isn't it a superb night.'

'Yeah, it is a great night,' he said, raising his head, looking up at the sky. 'Crazy isn't it, after such a lousy day.'

The wind seemed to have died altogether and there was no longer a chill in the air. The black sky above them was filled with stars and fine, misty-grey clouds hovered around a half-moon.

'Too nice a night to spend with other people around,' she said softly.

'What did you have in mind?' he said, ready to agree with almost anything she suggested. Of all the things he wanted right at that moment, being alone with her ranked first, second and third.

She stopped on a dim street-corner and stood facing him, running her hands up across his chest.

'I just don't feel like sitting in a pub on a night like this.'

'Fine by me.'

She stood on her tiptoes, drew his head down with her hand and kissed him – a soft, brief brush of her lips that made a silent sigh pass through his chest.

Magic, he thought.

In love.

'I know a lovely place, with a beautiful view of Loch

Aragarr,' she said drawing her head back. 'There's a beautiful little log shelter ... no one goes there at this time of the year.'

'You're the tour director,' he said holding her eyes with his.

'We could get a bottle of wine at the pub and just ... sip wine and watch the stars and the moonlight on the loch.'

'OK,' he said and noticed his voice had grown husky.

They strolled along the street, found a pub, bought a bottle of wine and headed back towards the car, not speaking much now, just holding each other, his arm around her shoulder, hers around his waist. They had gone beyond talking now, he knew, into a place where communication was carried out by eyes, smiles, the feel of skin through fabric.

It occurred to him that he was moving into unchartered territory, into a place as unfamiliar to him as Greenland or the Andaman Islands. But instantly he knew that was wrong, knew it was something else. It was just that he had forgotten what real human contact was, what it was like to be with someone he really cared about, someone with whom he just seemed to ...

To what?

To belong, to be right with; someone who seemed as if she was meant to be there.

When they got back to the car, he said: 'Mind if I drive? I haven't driven in this country yet.'

She didn't mind. 'Just make sure you stick to the right side of the road ... or should I say the left side of the road.'

'I won't forget, Scout's honour.'

They hardly spoke as they headed back towards Aragarr. She gave him directions in a near-whisper as if there was some kind of bubble around them she didn't want to burst, her hand holding the side of his coat, resting on his legs, as if she had to hold on to him, have some kind of contact with him.

As they swung around the eastern end of the loch, she said: 'Turn off's about a mile on. Slow down or I might miss it. I ... '

'Dammit,' he said, interrupting her.

'What's the matter?'

'We don't have a corkscrew for the wine.'

'Oh yes we do,' she said with a mischievous little girl's smile. She flipped open the glove box, thrust her hand inside, said 'Hey presto' and produced a knife with dozens of attachments, holding it up between two fingers like a lawyer showing exhibit one to the jury. 'With this I can open a wine bottle or a tin of beans or a beer bottle, there's a knife, a spoon, a fork. This is the ultimate knife. It's guaranteed to do anything.'

'Repair a nuclear missile?'

'Child's play.'

'Turn water into wine, base metal into gold?'

'Easily. Give me a hard one.'

'Prise open the heart of a cop who's forgotten how beautiful women can be?'

The mischievous smile softened. 'It might need a little help for that.'

Suddenly she swung her head around and yelled: 'Slow down, we're almost there. Yes, there it is, turn in there.'

He swung into a narrow road that ran between two stone pillars which were all that was left of what had once been a big gate.

'Go slowly,' she said. 'I've only been here once before, when I discovered this place ... and that was during the day.' She peered through the windscreen, leaning forward. 'Yes ... yes,' she said slowly, then, 'Yes, there it is. There's the shelter.'

The single knock on the door startled Malcolm out of his daydream. He put down the sandwich he had been eating and listened. The knock was not repeated.

His brow furrowed. It hadn't really been like a knock at all, more a slap with an open hand, or a bump.

He snapped the television set off – he hadn't really been watching it anyway, just keeping it on for company – and listened again, standing up. Then he walked through the hotel to the front door and drew it open.

At first, he didn't see anything. He was about to shut the door when he saw the cat, a black shape a few feet away, green eyes glowing.

'So it's you is it?' he said, 'go on ... away you go.'

The cat arched its back and hissed.

'Get away.' Malcolm stamped his foot. 'Go on.'

The cat padded towards him, then crouched near his feet, its tiny teeth bared, hissing and spitting, its right forepaw snatching at the air.

'Away you go.'

Malcolm didn't like to admit it to himself but it sent a cold shiver up his spine.

Afraid. Of a cat.

He was annoyed at himself and had started to close the door again when it jumped at him, screeching, clawing and biting. He yelled and slapped at it as claws ripped at his right thigh, tearing through his trousers, raking across his flesh. His hand struck a hard, warm body and the cat fell away and landed in the hall, its feet close together, its back instantly arching, the fur on the back of its neck standing on end.

'Get out.'

He poked a toe at it.

'Go on. Out.'

He touched his thigh with his hand and when he brought it away there was blood on his fingers.

'Out.'

He poked his toe at it again, trying to shove it out of the door. The cat snatched a paw across the leather toe-cap and screeched.

He winced as his thigh began to throb. It was as he bent forward and drew the torn cloth of his trousers aside to investigate the wound that the cat jumped again, clawing for his face. Instinctively he threw himself backwards, his heart jumping, unable to believe what was happening. Cats just didn't do this. A claw snatched open his shirt, tore four thin trenches across his chest.

He flailed at it, yelling, and one hand closed over the skin at the back of its neck. He flung it away down the entrance hall. It landed perfectly on all fours and trotted away, turning its head and glancing at him when it reached the stairs. Then it started up, leaping from one step to the next with a light thud.

Malcolm stared after it. He had been around cats all his life but he had never seen ...

Stop dreaming and get it out of the house, you silly man, said a voice in his head.

He grabbed an umbrella from a stand near the door, strode down the hall and started up the stairs, holding it like a sword.

That was when he noticed the odour that had started to fill the hall – the dead-flesh odour.

Just cat smell, he told himself. That was all.

But he knew it wasn't.

It was putrid, like something that had been dead for a very long time.

Twelve

The shelter that Janet had brought McBaith to was constructed of logs – a flat roof topping three windowless walls, a floor of bare planks, bench seats all the way round. There was no fourth wall – in its place they had a spectacular view of the rocky hillside that swept down to Loch Aragarr, the dark back of the loch itself, smeared with yellow moonlight, and the far bank crowded with ghostly birch trees.

Janet had taken a tartan rug from the boot of her car and spread it on the floor of the shelter and they had sat down, sipping the wine from paper cups Janet had found in her glove box and taking in the view, kissing softly and talking in whispers as if the night around them was a hallowed shrine they did not want to disturb.

Now they were no longer talking, no longer drinking the wine, no longer gazing down at the loch. Now there was no night, just each other. They lay tangled together on the crumpled rug, their kissing growing more passionate.

McBaith drew his head back when he heard the sound.

'What was that?' he murmured, lifting his mouth from hers.

'What?'

'That noise.'

She listened. 'I don't hear anything.'

'It's gone now,' he said after a moment.

As her lips found his again, he tried to recollect the sound. It had been like a hoarse sigh, constant for above five seconds. But there had been something more …

A crackling.

That was it.

An intermittent crackling, like an electrical sound. Her hand gripped the hair on the back of his neck and dragged his face more tightly against hers. Her lips were wide apart, wet on his face. Their teeth grated and he felt her tongue deep inside his mouth.

'Al,' she murmured, biting his neck, licking his throat. 'Al. How did ... this happen ... so quickly. I've never felt like this ... never.'

Her coat and jacket lay on the floor beside them and he found himself fumbling at the buttons on her blouse, his fingers brushing her soft flesh, the lace of her bra.

He stopped abruptly, lying quite still.

'What's wrong?' she said.

'There it is again.'

'What?'

'That noise. The same as before.'

She raised herself onto one elbow. 'I can't ... '

'Listen.' He lifted a finger into the air to silence her. 'It's like an electrical hum.'

'Maybe it's a power line?'

'No ... '

He sat up and his eyes darted down over the hillside to the loch. There was nothing out of the ordinary, nothing that hadn't been there before. Nothing had changed.

But the sound was getting louder.

'You're scaring me,' she said.

'Can't you hear it now?'

She cocked her head to one side then said slowly: 'Yes ... I ... what is it, Al?'

He let his gaze drift over the loch to the trees on the far bank, then sat up quickly, pointing.

'Look at that,' he yelled.

A ball of light – white tinged with pale blue – was whipping along the treetops, tumbling over and over.

She gripped his arm, 'What is it, Al?'

'You tell me.'

It was about a quarter of a mile away now but drawing closer all the time, rushing towards them.

'Is it ... ' She left the sentence unfinished.
'What?'
'No, it's silly.'
'What?'
'St Elmo's fire ... you know, what sailors see on the masts of ships sometimes.'

He shrugged, unable to take his eyes off the light. After a moment, he said: 'St Elmo's fire ... that's a kind of static electricity, isn't it?'

'I don't know.'

'Ball lightning,' he said thoughtfully. 'I think it's ball lightning.'

'Can it hurt us?'

He put his hand around her shoulders. 'I don't think so, I ... '

The ball of light reached the last line of trees on the far bank and began to descend through the branches of a tall birch.

McBaith realised he was gripping Janet's arm, digging his fingers into her flesh, hurting her, and let go quickly, aware that his palms were damp.

All the events of the day were dumped back into his mind like a heavy sack.

This wasn't some natural phenomenon. This wasn't ...

Wasn't right.

The ball of light appeared to hesitate at the treeline, hovering at the base of the tall birch then it shot forward and began to roll towards them over the waters of the loch.

Only three hundred yards away now, McBaith told himself. *Heading straight for us.*

Fear began to plough chilly furrows down the muscles of his back.

Two hundred yards.

'What the hell ... ' he heard himself say and felt Janet's hand gripping his.

He saw that the ball was bigger than he had realised, maybe ten feet by ten feet.

It reached the near bank and leapt up the slope, heading

straight for them. *A hundred yards away.*

'Let's get out of here,' he bawled.

He grabbed her hand, intending to stand up, to drag her away from that ...

That *thing*.

Fifty yards.

It was shooting across the ground now.

He was on his knees, his hands under Janet's arms, lifting her.

Thirty yards.

His eyes never left it. It was as if his head was nailed in that position.

Ten yards.

He was on his feet, crouched, pulling Janet up with urgent hands.

'Hurry ... It's ... it's ...

Suddenly an extreme drowsiness washed over him. It felt like his mind had been deep-frozen. He knew the light was all around them now, hovering there, but the drowsiness seemed to prevent him from questioning it, analysing it, trying to make sense of it.

Then he was aware he was on his back, staring up at the wooden ceiling.

How had he got there?

He knew he hadn't fallen.

Where was Janet?

Then he realised Janet was beside him, crouched over him. He saw two large, pale breasts with hard dark nipples and reached out to touch them.

Who had undressed her? Had he undressed her? Had she taken off her own clothes?

He couldn't remember anything after he had tried to stand up. Had he lost some time, had some kind of black-out?

Was ...

Her flesh felt so soft, yielding under the pressure of his fingertips. He ran his hands across her back and down to her legs. She was naked.

He closed his eyes as her mouth folded over his, her hair falling across his face. Then her lips moved to his neck and chest. When he opened his eyes, dragging his fingers through her silky hair, he saw that her skin was glowing with the same blue-white light of the ball that surrounded them. It was as if she had bathed in the light.

It seemed the most natural thing in the world.

It was so right.

He looked at his own arm and saw that it glowed too.

Dragging her face up to his, he kissed her again and they rolled over and over, off the rug, kissing, laughing, touching.

It was unbelievable. It was as if there was nothing in the world but her, as if nothing existed but sensation. He loved her, adored her, worshipped her. She was the world. She was the universe.

Then they were outside and the grass beneath them was soft and cool and the pleasure intensified.

He entered her and felt her body arching and jerking, tiny sharp sighs escaping from her lips.

When he climaxed it was like nothing before. A series of minute explosions ripped through him like a cluster of distant bombs going off one after the other. Colours of unimaginable intensity shot through his brain. He quivered from head to foot as shafts of pleasure leapt about his body.

He heard Janet scream and clutched at her, wanting to hold onto her forever.

'Al, Al, Al,' she moaned into his ear.

Then he opened his eyes.

The light was gone.

They were in the darkness, on the bare hillside, and a chill was nipping at his skin.

'What happened?' he said and shook her.

She opened her eyes and looked at him.

'What? Wow, did you slip something into that wine?'

She laughed nervously, shivering.

'It was the light, Janet. We were in the light. I don't remember how ... '

'Yes, I know ... '

He felt a sudden sense of danger, of being used, of being toyed with.

There *was* something in Aragarr. Something oh-so *wrong*.

They were all in danger.

Janet too.

Instantly he knew that the thing that he wanted least in the world was for something to happen to Janet. 'It was beautiful,' she said, 'but ... ' Her face was filled with confusion. 'It was like it wasn't just us ... like ... the light ... '

A shiver convulsed her body and she sat up, wrapping her arms about herself.

'Let's get back to Aragarr,' he said and helped her up.

Malcolm was sure he could hear the muffled patter of the cat's feet in the end bedroom. He stood by the slightly-ajar door, his ear turned to the opening. All the bedroom doors were open, all the rooms being aired, so the cat could have gone into any one. When he had first gone upstairs, he had believed he had heard movements in two other bedrooms but searches there had produced nothing.

But now he was certain.

He raised the umbrella, threw open the door and stepped into the room.

Nothing.

No sign of the cat. No muffled patter now.

He listened, standing absolutely still, but still he heard no sound.

He checked between a chest of drawers and the wall, under the bed, under the wardrobe.

It was as he turned back towards the door that he picked up a movement in the corner of his eye. He spun around and found himself staring at his own reflection in a mirror on the wall.

But something had moved ...

... and if it had been reflected in the mirror it must be behind him now.

He swung around and saw the black shape slip under the bed.

The cat. It *had* to be.

Yet it hadn't looked like a cat, hadn't moved like a cat. For one thing it had looked too big and for another it hadn't had any of a cat's animal fluidity. It had looked like a plastic bag of discarded rags sliding along the floor.

Sliding. Yes, that was what it had done. Slid, shifted. Not trotted or scampered or darted. Not like an animal at all.

But of course it was the cat, he told himself, and he had put up with this nonsense for long enough.

He dragged back the bedclothes, bent over and looked under the bed, holding the umbrella in front of him like a sword.

There was nothing there.

He knelt on one knee and let his eyes travel the length of the bed.

But there was just empty space. Nothing more.

Frowning, he raised his head.

And froze, his eyes staring.

He felt as if his heart had stopped beating.

On the far wall was a dark, indistinct shape, about the size of an overcoat. It was almost like a dirty mark on the wall but it moved, twitching and quivering.

He tried to stand up but it was as if his knee was glued to the floor. Fear moved through him like a chilled hand, gently exploring.

The dark shape became clearer, not moving so much now. It looked like a garment of some kind, like a heavy black dress or a monk's cassock.

And there was a face at the top.

No.

Not a face.

A skull, the faded outline of a skull.

He jumped to his feet now and stumbled back towards the door.

The skull trembled like an image on the surface of water, grew more indistinct, then was gone, replaced by a woman's head, bent forward, fair hair falling over the face. The head was a clearer image than the skull had been, he realised.

The thought came to him with startling clarity that it was as if the figure was an image projected into reality from another place, another time, an image struggling to find enough energy to be whole, to find its identity. It wasn't real, he told himself. It was just like a television picture.

Don't panic, a voice in his head yelled. Stay calm and get out.

Just as he drew the door open, the head began to tilt back, misty strands of fair hair falling back and separating, revealing the wavering image of an impassive face, a mocking smile playing on the lips. Only the eyes were clear, and they were cat's eyes, watching him, unblinking.

Filled with hate.

He threw the door open and ran, his heart jerking in his chest, cold shrapnel of terror slicing through him.

And he knew something was coming after him, following him along the upstairs hall. *Moving fast.*

He snatched at the banisters and propelled himself downstairs.

What if it caught him? What would happen? What was it? What did it want with him?

It was certain to catch him. It ...

Then he heard the front door opening.

Al.

It *had* to be Al.

Please let it be Al.

'Al,' he yelled. 'Al, is that you?'

He could see the door now. Janet Ritchie coming in. Al behind her.

Thank God. *Thank God.*

Relief surged through him.

He stumbled down the last couple of steps and staggered along the hall, grabbing for McBaith, holding his shoulders.

'A cat,' he yelled. 'And there was ... like a woman up there ... and ... '

'Calm down, Malcolm.'

The old man looked into McBaith's face, trying desperately to find the words to explain. Then he realised McBaith was looking beyond him, down the hall.

The woman?

Was she *there?*

He spun around just as the cat darted past his legs and leapt out into the night.

'Not a cat, Al,' he shouted, tugging at McBaith's arms. 'Go after it. You'll see. Not ... '

McBaith turned out the door and scanned the street. He spotted the cat away to his right and sprinted after it.

It shot across the street and disappeared down the wooden stairway to the beach. As he approached, he could hear its paws padding rhythmically on the steps.

He reached the stairway, grabbed the wooden handrail and clattered down to the beach, his eyes searching the dull pools of light from the street lamps which seemed to make patches of the sand glow.

There was no sign of the cat, no sound except the sigh of the sea.

He hurried back to the hotel and found Janet and Malcolm in the smoking-room.

Malcolm had his face in his hands. 'It was a terrible thing to see,' he was saying. 'The woman's eyes weren't the eyes of a human. They were the eyes of the cat.'

He parted his fingers and looked through them into the fire, as if reliving his horror. He seemed to be unaware that McBaith had come into the room. His face was slack, heavy and scared.

McBaith looked at Janet, raising his eyebrows questioningly, and she outlined everything Malcolm had told her.

McBaith sat down opposite Malcolm and said: 'What did the woman look like?'

'She was wearing ... like a black robe of heavy cloth. She had fair hair and ... I don't want to say any more.'

'What? Why?'

'If I'm going to accuse someone, I want to be very sure about what I'm saying.'

'Accuse someone. You mean ... you recognised her?'

'I'm not sure. I can't be certain. Mischievous tongues can cause a lot of trouble. I keep my thoughts to myself unless I'm sure about what I'm saying.'

'I understand that, Malcolm, but ... '

Malcolm raised tired eyes to McBaith and said: 'It was as if something was mocking me, taunting me, as if it could hurt me whenever it wanted to but just wanted to scare me. I ... There was such an overwhelming feeling of evil. Al, that feeling of black evil has been in Aragarr these last two weeks. I know you don't believe in that kind of thing but it's here. You can laugh if you like ... '

'I'm not laughing, Malcolm, not any more. But you have to tell me who you think you saw.'

'No, I ... '

'Was it Meg Rees?'

There was a hush in the room after he spoke, a silence beyond silence. Malcolm blinked and his eyes said 'yes' but he remained silent, watching McBaith.

'Was it?' McBaith insisted.

'I'll not take the chance of falsely accusing anyone.'

'But you think it was?'

'Aye.'

'OK,' McBaith said with a note of finality.

'What are you going to do?' Janet said.

'Do? I'm going to find out what's going on here.'

'How?'

'I don't know ... but I know where I'm going to start.'

'Where?' Malcolm said.

'I'm going to eat humble pie and talk to Annie Stewart.' He paused then said: 'Malcolm, if it's all right by you I want Janet to spend the night here at the hotel. And tomorrow I want us all to stick together. I know we're in danger ... all of us. I want both of you with me.'

Janet started to say something but McBaith held up a hand. 'I want you here in the hotel tonight.'

She nodded slowly. 'All right.'

'I'll get a room ready,' Malcolm said, standing up.

'We'll go and see Annie first thing in the morning,' McBaith said. Malcolm was leaving the room when he added: 'Do you have a torch?'

'Yes.'

'Could I borrow it?'

There were a lot of questions in Malcolm's eyes but he just said, 'Of course' and turned away down the hall.

McBaith took Janet in his arms. 'Just get to bed and get as much sleep as you can,' he said, then held her tightly.

Malcolm returned a moment later with the torch.

'Thanks,' McBaith said. 'You two get to bed. I'll be back in a minute. There's something I want to check.'

Back on the beach, at the bottom of the stairway where the cat had disappeared, he began to search the sand. At first he found nothing, just bare sand rippled by the waves of high-tide. No sign of the cat, no sign of anything.

Then he saw it.

Ten feet from the bottom step.

A single human footprint, fresh and clear. The imprint of a small bare foot.

He studied it for a moment, crouched on the sand, then walked on.

A few feet away he found another, then another, set wide apart.

The footprints of a woman running.

McBaith found it hard to get to sleep. He lay awake, the light off, his mind teeming with questions. He had just glanced at the luminous dial on his watch and seen that it was almost three o'clock when the door of his room opened gently.

He raised himself onto his elbow and saw that it was Janet, dressed in one of Malcolm's pyjama jackets.

'I was scared,' she said. 'I couldn't sleep.'

He drew the bedclothes back and she slipped quickly in beside him. It felt so right when he wrapped his arms about her, holding her against him. It felt like it was meant to be, like every day of his life had been leading up to his meeting with this woman.

When sleep finally did come McBaith dreamed of a great flickering light and the light seemed to be beckoning to him, inviting him in. When he went closer he found that the light was really millions of tiny particles. Like exquisite diamonds.

The urge to step into the light was overwhelming but he held back.

It was as if he knew the light was an illusion, a tempting bait at the mouth of a trap, and that beyond it lay something dark and terrible.

Thirteen

Annie Stewart was dreaming too.

In her dream, the heads of dead men came to dance around her bed, skulls with tiny patches of scalp and hair and dried-up flesh, lipless mouths frozen in everlasting grins, empty eye sockets that seemed to mock her.

She got out of bed in the dream and was led by skeletal hands through the village (but it wasn't Aragarr, not her Aragarr, not with the masted ships in the harbour and the great Roundhouse and the empty space where the sea wall now stood),

Then she saw a great crowd and they were gathered around a huge fire and flames licked high into the night, scarlet against moonless black. There were two people in the fire, tied to tree branches thrust into the ground, vague shapes beyond the tormenting flames. Annie knew one was a woman because although she could not see her clearly the woman's screams sliced through the night with such intensity that they brought tears to Annie's eyes.

Why was this happening?

The crowd around her shouted at the two who had been sentenced to death, howling their hate.

Then the wind snatched at the flames, parting them, and Annie saw the face of a man with a long scar on his forehead. He yelled defiantly, laughing as the flames quivered across the black robe he wore, bit into his flesh.

Annie froze when she heard the words the man said, froze with the knowledge that she now possessed.

She knew. Now she *knew*. Nothing was hidden from her. But could she live with that knowing? Would she be allowed to live? She pushed frantically through the crowd and grasped the skeletal hands which she knew would lead her back to her bedroom, back to her time.

But there was another there now, in the darkness beyond the dancing heads, and she recognised the face that watched the burnings with anguish.

She hurried on, desperate that the woman did not see her. When the woman's face began to turn in her direction, she jerked her eyes away, ducked her head down.

Then she sat up in bed.

Had she been brought back by the dancing skulls or ...

Was this still the dream?

Her flesh felt as if it was burning and she whipped back the bedclothes.

A tiny flame, no bigger than that on a match, flickered about the fabric at the bottom of her nightgown.

Did she have to bother with it? This was still the dream, wasn't it? Just an illusion, like when her face had been burning the day before?

Then the flame nipped at her flesh and smoke bit at her nostrils.

Not a dream? Not illusion?

She snatched up her leg and slapped at the flame until it was gone.

Instantly, she felt a burning pain behind her knee. She dragged off her nightgown and saw a pale flame licking along the fair hairs on the back of her right leg.

Spontaneous combustion.

The words jumped into her mind as she slapped the flame out.

Something was going to *burn her*.

She was going to be burned alive.

But was it dream or no dream? Illusion or reality? Would she awake from this?

Was she in her Aragarr?

Something nipped at her left thigh, like a hot brand. She felt a flame running up over her belly. Searing heat gnawed at her armpits.

She was dangerous...

Because she *knew*. *Because of what she had seen.*

Therefore she was going to be killed. She leapt off the bed, hands flailing at the flames, and caught a glimpse of dawn breaking through the window, yellow light bleeding over the tops of the pine trees above the village, eating away the shadows around the houses of Aragarr.

Her Aragarr.

It was real. Not a dream. Not illusion.

She slapped at her stomach, tried to crush the fire under her armpits.

Then a great flame enveloped her with a whispering whooosh and she fell back onto the bed.

DAY of the five.

Day of THE FIVE

DAY OF THE FIVE.

The words shrieked at McBaith from darkness – a woman's voice, exultant, triumphant.

Terrifying.

He opened his eyes and it was as if he was in a well, the light of day ...

(of sanity)

... high above him. He reached out for it, his fingers white against the blackness, but it was too far.

DAY OF THE FIVE.

Get to the light ...

Get to ...

Then fingers groped over his body, grabbing his arm. His muscles quivered then froze into solid blocks and he pulled violently away from the fingers, his mind frantic with naked fear.

Had to get to the light.

But it was getting smaller.

He was falling away from it.

DAY OF THE FIVE.

Then another voice. 'Al ... Al ... wake up ... '

His eyes weren't open ...

He had ...

He jerked them open and found himself in his bed, sitting up, his body matted in chilled perspiration. Janet was beside him, an arm over his shoulder.

'Today is the day ... of the five,' he muttered.

'What?' she said, then rubbed the back of his neck, caressed his hair. 'You were having a dream, Al, that's all.'

He looked at her, the memory of the words and the dark place whipping away into a corner of his subconscious.

'Some dream,' he said slowly, heavily.

It was seven-thirty when McBaith shook Malcolm awake. He and Janet were up, dressed and ready to leave. Malcolm took ten minutes to get ready and then they headed for Annie Stewart's house. It was behind the High Street, at the end of a short track, a small stone cottage with green shutters.

There were four cars parked in the track when they drove up in Janet's car and a group of people were gathered around the front door.

'What's happening?' Malcolm said to an elderly woman who was standing near the front door.

'There's been an accident, Malcolm,' she said. 'Annie's been badly burned. Mrs McGhee, you know the one who used to be a nurse, she's with her now and the ambulance is on its way. Doctor Dunbar isn't here. He's visiting his son in Glasgow, I ... '

McBaith didn't hear any more. He ducked through the low front door and hurried through the house until he found the bedroom.

Neil Ritchie was standing in the doorway and he greeted McBaith with a solemn nod. 'You'd better not come in, Al, it's ... '

McBaith pushed passed him.

There were three other people in the room – William Macpherson, a woman McBaith guessed was the ex-nurse and a short, powerfully-built man McBaith had never seen before.

Annie lay on the bed, a hideous sight, her skin charred and blackened, raw and bleeding in places, burned to the bone in others. The ex-nurse was applying some kind of ointment and most of Annie's body glistened with it. The sheet beneath her was singed around her body but otherwise untouched.

'We can't make sense of it, Al,' Macpherson said. 'She was burned on the bed and yet the bed didn't go up. It's as if the flames came from her own body.'

'Has she said anything?'

'Said anything?'

'Yeah.'

'We just got here. Mrs McGhee has been with Annie since she was found about twenty minutes ago.'

The woman nodded to McBaith: 'She's been babbling ... not making much sense.'

Annie groaned and the ragged black eyelids flicked open and beckoned to McBaith.

When McBaith knelt down beside the bed, Annie muttered 'Not in the world of men' and her body trembled with a thin laugh. The other men in the room moved forward, as if drawn by the hoarse, rasping words that seemed to be spoken through a rusted pipe, from far away.

'I'll be lifting ... my face to ... my God soon,' she said. 'With all my sins there beside me ... accusing me ... '

'Don't talk now, Annie,' the ex-nurse said.

'Must ... must talk now ... '

A blackened hand gripped McBaith's sleeve and Annie's eyes moved around the men in the room. A tiny nod and a weak smile greeted Malcolm's arrival. The eyes glazed for a moment then cleared and the thin body quivered with pain.

Annie gritted her teeth and a word slipped from her lips.

'Seer,' she said.

'What?' McBaith leaned forward. 'What did you say?'

'Seer ... I know what's ... bringing the evil ... to Aragarr. Seer. Aragarr Seer.'

'Who ... '

'Trying to destroy village ... vengeance ... '

The grip on McBaith's sleeve grew tighter, as if the old woman was clinging onto life itself.

'Must ... tell ... There is ... communicant here ...

drawing in the evil. Growing stronger. Here today like never before. More evil now. Communicant must die ... maid of the seer.'

'Who is it, Annie?' Malcolm said.

'My soul ... near to going before the Lord ... must not die with blood ... of innocent on me.'

'Who is it?' McBaith persisted.

'Without communicant ... evil cannot prevail ... not person ... have no mercy ... '

'Who?'

'Swear ... all of you ... that if I speak ... the name ... ' She coughed and the charred body jerked horribly. 'You will not act ... until ... you are certain. She mustn't die because of words ... from my lips. I'm not ... positive.'

'Who?' Malcolm said.

'Meg ... Rees ... is maid of the ... seer. Cannot ... swear before ... God I am sure. She carried his ... name. Evil ... ' Her words dropped to a tiny whisper and they strained to hear. 'Evil ... reverse of ... good. Reverse of Rees ... '

'Seer,' Macpherson said.

'Meg ... not of earth ... but be sure ... I beg you ... no innocent blood ... on my hands.'

'We promise, Annie, we'll be sure.'

McBaith felt as if he was the only person in the room who didn't know what was going on. He was looking from one face to the other when the ambulancemen entered the room, gently lifted Annie onto a stretcher and rushed her away.

'What was she talking about?' McBaith said at last, his patience ragged.

'The Black Seer of Aragarr,' Macpherson said. His words seemed hollow, as if spoken in an echo chamber.

'Who?'

Malcolm said: 'He was a man with the gift of second sight but he abused it. They said he sold his gift and his soul to the devil. That's all I know. People in Aragarr never talked about him very much.'

'His name was Kenneth McBaith,' Macpherson said.

'McBaith.' McBaith spoke his own name and it seemed strange on his lips.

'Yes,' Malcolm said. 'There was a time when McBaith was a common name in Aragarr. You could say he was a distant relative of ours.'

McBaith felt as if he was losing a grip on what was being said.

'Hold on just a minute,' he said. 'What we're talking about here is a ... seer ... a dead man ... who has come back ... for what? Vengeance? Isn't that what Annie said. Is that what we're seriously talking about?'

Nobody answered.

'Why vengeance?'

'He was burned by the people of the town,' Malcolm said, 'and his ashes scattered from the end of The Rock. That's all I know. People in Aragarr don't talk about him very often. He was hated here in his time, by the village, even by his family.'

'What did he look like?' McBaith said quietly. Suddenly he was thinking about the hideous face in the Roundhouse, about the bloodshot eyes that had seemed to mesmerise him.

The men shrugged.

'Did he swear some kind of vengeance on the village?'

'Not much is known about him, Al,' Malcolm said. 'Every old place has someone terrible in their history but after two hundred years who remembers what they might have said?'

'Do you swallow any of this?'

Malcolm sighed. 'I don't know any more.'

'What's this about Meg being the seer's maid and what's a communicant?'

Malcolm shook his head as if to say he had run out of answers and Macpherson said: 'Annie meant someone who is in communion with ... evil forces. Meg's here to draw them in.'

'That's why she must die,' the fourth man in the room said.

'Hold it right there,' McBaith said severely, chopping a hand through the air as if to cut off the man's words.

'It's not your business or your village, McBaith,' the man said angrily.

'I know, but ... ' McBaith began.

Malcolm interrupted, saying: 'That's Jack Andrews, Al. Fiona's father.'

McBaith let the surge of anger that had leapt up inside him subside then said: 'Nobody's getting killed. Let's find out more.'

'I say she dies before anyone else gets hurt,' Andrews said.

McBaith ignored him, turning to Malcolm. 'I'm in uncharted waters here, Malcolm. I don't know what's going on. Whatever it turns out to be I don't think it's going to make sense to me ... but nobody is going get killed.'

'She's a communicant,' Andrews said, 'not a person at all.'

'Can you control this guy?' McBaith said to Malcolm. 'Just give me time to find out more, to talk to Meg.'

Malcolm nodded and Macpherson gave Andrews a severe glance and said: 'We'll wait.'

'OK,' McBaith said. If I wanted to find out everything I can about this seer where would I find books, documents?'

'They could be anywhere,' Malcolm said. 'Library, museum ... the seer wasn't a folk hero we all wanted to know about. Most of the people here have probably never heard the seer's name mentioned more than once in their lives.'

'Try Arran Hay,' Macpherson said. 'He's the librarian at Aultglen. That's our nearest library.'

'Thanks.'

As he left the room, McBaith took Malcolm by the arm and drew him after him. In the hall, he said: 'Try to keep Andrews away from Meg and try to keep this quiet. Give me a couple of hours to poke around. I don't want any lynch mobs. Oh and ... stay with people. Don't go back to the hotel alone. See you.'

Striding to the car, he said to Janet: 'Get me to Meg's house, will you?'

'Certainly. But ... I saw Annie and ... '

As they drove up the hill, he outlined what had happened.

'I've never heard of the Aragarr Seer,' she said. 'Do you really ... '

'I don't know,' he said savagely, biting off her sentence. 'I just know there's danger. I know that for sure.'

At Meg's house, McBaith hammered on the door for a long time while Janet peered through the windows. There was no sign of life. McBaith found an unlocked window and they climbed in. It was chilly in the house and McBaith found himself thinking it was so cold no-one could have slept there the night before. He checked the bedroom and found the bed neatly made.

The house was sparsely furnished and McBaith guessed Meg Rees had rented it furnished and brought none of her own things. What struck him as not making sense was the fact that he saw no tools for making jewellery, no workbench, no raw materials. There was a shed behind the cottage but a glance inside showed it was empty.

An old black telephone hung on the wall in the kitchen and McBaith cradled the receiver on his shoulder while he looked up the number of the Aultglen library.

He dialled and a voice answered on the second ring.

'Arran Hay,' he said.

'Speaking.'

'My name's McBaith. I was told you might be able to help me. I'm trying to get some information about the Aragarr Seer. I thought you might have some books about him. He was ... '

'I know who he was, Mr McBaith. The only book we have is *The Black Seer*.'

'That's about Kenneth McBaith is it?'

'Yes, but it's a novel.'

'A novel. I need information. You don't have any documents or ... '

'Swinton MacLean has all the papers relating to the seer. He's a writer. He wrote *The Black Seer* after buying all the papers at the Laurie Estate auction fifteen years ago.'

'Where do I find him?'

'Where are you now?'

'Aragarr.'

'Then it's simple. He lives just behind Aultglen. You can't miss it ... the big white cottage on the hill overlooking the village.'

McBaith covered the receiver with his hand and said to Janet: 'How far is Aultglen.'

'Eight miles or so.'

'Thanks for all your help,' McBaith said into the receiver and hung up.

'Ever heard of Swinton MacLean?' he said as he leafed through the phone book.

'No.'

'A writer.'

'No.'

McBaith dialled again. This time the phone rang for a long time. He was about to hang up when a voice said: 'Hello.'

Swinton MacLean was helpful but his slow way of speaking irritated McBaith. He found himself interrupting the writer again and again. Yes, MacLean said, he had the papers. Documents, book, letters that referred to the seer. Of course McBaith was welcome to see them. Most of the original material relating to the seer, including a book written in 1826 called *Man of the Devil, an account of the life of the Black Seer*, had been destroyed by fire but in 1886 Sir Roland Marlow had taken all the records then available and written *Not in God's Domain*. This contained reproductions of some plates which had appeared in the earlier book but survived the fire.

Was McBaith doing some kind of research? MacLean asked.

McBaith hesitated then said: 'I'd like to see the material now if that's OK. It's not research exactly, I'll explain when I get there.'

'It sounds mysterious, Mr McBaith.'

'It's very important.'

'All right. I'd be glad to help. I've been thinking of handing the papers over to a museum. I believe ... '

'See you soon,' McBaith interrupted and hung up.

McBaith drove while Janet sat silently beside him, her hands clasped tightly in her lap. Fear, he thought, she's afraid. But he wouldn't let anything happen to her, couldn't let anything happen to her. After finding her he couldn't lose her now.

A mile along the main road, heading north, he slowed the car and looked down at her.

'Did you feel that?' he said.

'What?'

'Didn't you feel anything?'

'No.'

'Twice since I've been in Aragarr I've had a weird sensation. It's like that feeling before a storm when the air seems heavy, thick, like it could choke you, you know. It came and went. But today I've had that feeling all day, as if Aragarr's filled with it.'

'Maybe a storm is coming.'

'No. Because just back there it stopped suddenly, it just disappeared. That's why I asked you if you felt anything. It was like we went through an invisible curtain and instantly there wasn't any heaviness anymore.'

'I didn't feel anything.'

He looked back down the hill, searching for Aragarr, but it was hidden behind the trees now.

'It's as if something has closed around Aragarr,' he said.

Laurie Murdoch woke with a start and went downstairs to make her breakfast, mumbling irritatedly to herself.

She had lived in the same cottage on the banks of the Aragarr Burn for all of her ninety years – she had come into the world in the upstairs bedroom, reared four children in the house and had forty years of married life without ever considering the possibility of living anywhere else.

Now she lived alone, hardly ever going beyond her front door unless it was pension day and there was shopping to be done. Her life had been a peaceful one with no dramatic events or tragedies, no great successes, no great failures, no astounding peaks or terrible troughs. It had been an everyday life with nothing to make it very different from the lives of a thousand other women. She always said she had no complaints and would be happy to 'go to the Lord' when her time came.

But in the past fortnight or so something had changed. She couldn't put her finger on what it was but it was as if there was something new in Aragarr, as if something ...

(something *nasty*, she thought on the occasions when she tried to analyse it.)

... had moved in and occupied the place. It was as powerful as a bad smell and as painful as a grazed knee yet it was nothing physical.

Laurie was as much a part of Aragarr as the earth and the stones of the houses and the bones in the old churchyard across the road. If anything happened in the village she sensed it like a radio antenna picking up a faint signal, like a mother sensing that her child was ill.

As she ate, she realised the feeling was stronger now than ever before.

She finished her breakfast, climbed the stairs and started to make the bed.

That was when she heard the yell — the voice of a youth, hoarse and exultant — and hurried to her window.

She saw the boys immediately, two youths of sixteen or seventeen running about the graveyard.

Playing football.

Kicking their ball and dodging about the gravestones.

Such a thing was unthinkable.

She jerked open the window and shouted: 'Hey. You boys get away from the kirkyard this instant.'

They ignored her for a moment and she shouted again: 'Hey. You heard me. That's no place to play football.'

Then one of them turned and looked blankly at her. She knew him, it was Tom Law's boy, but he looked different. His head was held low, his youthful face slack, the eyes hooded.

He began to laugh but it wasn't a boy's laugh. No. Not a cheeky laugh or a defiant chuckle such as she might have expected.

It was something else altogether, crude and coarse, like that of an angry drunk.

She slammed the window shut, suddenly frightened.

The boy turned away as the ball trundled towards him and she saw him bend over and pick it up.

Then he was facing her again, holding the ball up so that she could see it, showing it to her.

And she saw that it was a skull and that clots of earth still clung to it.

Fourteen

The first thing McBaith noticed about Swinton MacLean was that he had a smear of grey dust on his nose. There was more dust on the sleeve of his shirt and on his trousers.

'I haven't found all the papers you want,' MacLean said as he led them into the house. 'I've been up in the attic searching for them ... that's why I'm so filthy.' He clapped his hands and rubbed them together as if to remove some grime. 'I'm sure I'll find them in a minute. In the meantime, I've put all the papers I have found on my desk, over there.'

The desk wasn't really a desk – it was a huge table set in front of a picture window that looked down over Aultglen.

'If you'd given me more time, I'd have had the papers ready.'

He was a small man with blue, eager-to-please eyes and the look of a person who spends too much time alone and is always delighted to have company.

'There seems to be some urgency about what you're doing,' he observed. 'Care to tell me what's going on?'

McBaith gave him a toned-down version of some of the things that had been happening in Aragarr.

'I know how crazy it looks ... thinking the things we're thinking,' he said when he had finished, 'but when you've seen the things we've seen, you begin to doubt ... just about everything.'

'There are worlds beyond worlds,' MacLean said thoughtfully then added: 'I'll get on with my search then. I'm sure I can find the other material, it's just a question of time. I wrote *The Black Seer* fifteen years ago, you see. I haven't had the papers out since then.'

As he disappeared up a stairway, McBaith sat down at the table.

'What are we looking for exactly?' Janet said.

'I don't know. Anything.'

She stood behind him, resting her hand on his shoulder, as he began to flick through letters that covered the period from 1780 to 1890 about prophecies by the Aragarr Seer. There was nothing of any relevance and he started ploughing through a heap of MacLean's notes about prophecies which had been fulfilled in modern times.

'From our seas will come black water richer than gold,' the seer had foretold and alongside the quote MacLean had scribbled 'oil'. 'There will come a day when there is more Scots blood across the water than in the land of our ancestors' read another quote and MacLean had written 'True' beside it.

McBaith grunted and continued to scan the sheets. 'Many of our nation will die in the great fire of war when a violent man of destiny comes to rule over Europe in the year 1949.' He hadn't been far out with his Hitler prophecy, McBaith thought. 'The day of the horse will pass and there will come wagons belching smoke.' 'Remember the magic seven for I will come again when one of my blood returns from far away. He will be the seventh son of a seventh son and will fulfil his destiny.'

McBaith stiffened, cold fingers scampering across his shoulders.

He was a McBaith and a seventh son.

He had come from far away.

His father had had four brothers but he had once mentioned another two who had died in infancy.

'What is it, Al?' Janet said.

'Nothing,' he said quickly.

Why? Why hadn't he told her?

It couldn't mean anything, could it? Not *really?*

The questions that had been plaguing him all day began to multiply in his mind, like eager bacilli in warm flesh. Questions about his going-home feeling and his thin apprehensive fear, his indescribable sense of destiny and the numbers that kept leaping into his brain in dreams, the man he had seen in the Roundhouse and what had happened to him and Janet the night before.

He turned the sheet over quickly and found himself looking at a photocopy of a drawing. In the top right-hand corner, in minute type, were the words 'The Sign of the Seer'

The drawing was simple – a dark circle with two white upright crescents back to back in the centre.

He sighed then looked at Janet and said quietly: 'It's the same as your necklace.'

'Yes, the one I bought from Meg.'

She tugged it out of her blouse and looked from it to the drawing and back again.

'Identical,' he said.

Janet started to say something but MacLean came back into the room carrying a couple of exercise books, a pile of dusty, browning notepaper and an ancient, broken-backed book with a blue cover.

'I've found some more material,' he said. 'Sir Roland Marlow's book was right at the bottom of my trunk. Of course you must remember that he wrote his account a century after the seer's death and mostly from other people's memories of having read the earlier work, *Man of the Devil, an account of the life of the Black Seer*. It's rather like me writing about Waterloo from what people are telling me about books they read about it. We'll never know the full truth now. I ... '

'Mr MacLean. I'm not sure I've got time to go through all this. It could take me a week. Would you mind answering a couple of questions?'

'Not at all.'

'Was there someone in the seer's life called Meg?'

'Oh yes. Meggy, she was called. She played a large part in the drama. She started as his maid. They say she was a girl of purity and innocence who was corrupted by the seer. She took part in many vile rituals ... some of which were said to have given the seer his famous power over the animals of the glens and forests. She was imprisoned with him after his first arrest. They escaped, you know, the seer and his wife and Meggy.'

'No, I didn't. Go on.'

'After the escape, Meggy was used as a sacrifice by the seer in some devilish ritual ... but they say she loved him to the last. There's a plate of Meggy in Roland Marlow's book. It was all that survived the fire that destroyed all copies of the earlier work.'

MacLean put the book down in front of McBaith and McBaith began to flick through the pages.

'It's near the back,' MacLean said. 'You can actually see the burn marks that were on the original. Of course the earlier work had plates of drawings of the seer and his wife and ... '

MacLean kept talking but McBaith wasn't listening any more. The book had fallen open at a sketch of a young girl with a wistful smile. The picture was faded and the top left-hand corner of the face blurred and darkened where fire had scorched the original but there was no doubt who it was.

The girl that looked up at him was Meg Rees.

No-one spoke for a moment then McBaith said: 'There's a quote in your notes about the seer returning ... something about the magic seven and the seventh son of a seventh son ... '

'Yes. He said that just before he died, when they burned him. He was dragged from the Roundhouse ... that was like a prison ... '

'Yeah, I know ... But I thought you said he escaped.'

'That was the first time he was imprisoned. He was caught again, after he had killed Meg. The people were so incensed at Meg's death that they dragged out the seer and his wife and burned them at the stake.'

'What else did he say ... when he talked about coming back?'

'Oh there's a full account in Roland Marlow's book. Chapter fifteen, I believe. Very dramatic stuff indeed.'

As McBaith began to thumb through the book, MacLean said:

'Would you both like some tea?'
'Thank you, yes,' Janet said.
'I'd kill for a cup of coffee,' McBaith said.
'One tea, one coffee, coming up.'

McBaith found chapter fifteen and began to speed read his way through the details of the seer's capture – 'the beast McBaith' Marlow called him. It was hard going because Marlow wrote in a long-winded, complex manner with seventy-word sentences and page-long paragraphs. More often than not, he used ten or twenty words when one would have done, convoluted phrases when it would have been easier to state the facts simply. McBaith guessed that was how things were done in the 1880s.

He knew MacLean had retreated to the kitchen and was aware that the writer was whistling but he read for several minutes before he realised what the tune was. It was the lilting, sad melody he had been whistling when he had arrived in Aragarr.

He raised his eyes from the book and Janet said: 'What is it?'

'Shshsh,' he said listening. Then he stood up and walked stiffly into the kitchen.

MacLean flashed him a smile.

'That tune,' McBaith said. 'It's an old Aragarr tune, isn't it?'

'Ah, you know it.'

'You could say that.'

'You coming here brought it to mind. When I was researching *The Black Seer* I spoke to all the older people around Aragarr, to see if they had any stories to tell about the seer ... you know, the kind of thing their parents might have told them. Amazing how few of them knew anything about the seer ... '

'Tell me about the tune,' McBaith said impatiently.

'One of the farmers hummed me a tune, that tune. He said his grandfather had told him it was called "The Song of the Seer".'

Andy Blair was ten years old and what his teachers and his parents called a dreamer. Occasionally Andy lived in the small West Scotland village of Aragarr but most of the time he was somewhere else – piloting a space craft in a distant galaxy, marching with the legions of ancient Rome, playing football and scoring a sensational goal while eighty thousand fans chanted his name, hurtling through a forest in a rally car, dive-bombing the army of some terrible tyrant or involved in some equally fascinating drama conjured up by his imagination.

Sitting alone in his room after breakfast that morning he was in a time warp. He had been transported to a terrifying period in the future when soldiers without faces rounded everyone up and dropped them into a bottomless pit. The soldiers and their leaders and all the bad people wore the same insignia on their uniforms – a dark blue circle with white back-to-back crescents.

Even as the drama unfolded, he thought the insignia was odd because the day before he had seen it in two of his daydreams – it had been on a rally car he had been driving and on a Roman legion standard.

Funny thing that.

As he began to tire of being chased by soldiers without faces and watching people being dropped into the bottomless pit, the daydream faded and finally disappeared as if it had been a bubble and someone had stuck a pin in it. He stood up and walked to his window. His absently wandering eyes immediately picked up a movement beyond the treeline, two hundred yards up the hill, and he stared at the spot.

Then he saw the foxes, five of them trotting up to the treeline and stopping there, looking down at the village.

A moment later, further along the treeline, he saw a group of weasels and a couple of wild cats.

This was interesting. It didn't make any sense but it was fascinating nevertheless. It was as if the animals were the advance scouts of some invading army which was about to assemble on the hill, he thought, just as he saw the shaggy figures of three wild goats scrambling through some bushes and two mink seated at the base of a tall birch tree.

A great stag came next, plodding through the brush and taking up a position among the foxes.

Then he saw the pair of golden eagles. They soared above the treetops, banked and dropped to a branch above the mink.

One of the eagles seemed to look straight at him, its hunter's eyes glaring. He jumped when it gave a loud, sharp cry ...

(as if to warn the other creatures they were being watched, he thought)

... then he began to imagine he had a rifle and was raising it slowly to his shoulder. He would put a single shot through the eagle's breast and have it stuffed.

The eagle screeched again, a longer, angrier sound this time.

Fifteen

MacLean set the coffee beside McBaith's elbow just as he reached the section in chapter fifteen when the seer and his wife were being dragged from the Roundhouse.

'Thanks,' he said, taking a sip and flipping over a page.

He read: 'In the light of the great burning torches held high by the mob, hell bent on doing their duty to their God and humanity, the seer's countenance was like that of the devil, his master, to whom his soul had been given in bondage for all time. His eyes did glitter like a beast of the pit and the scar on his forehead was alive and glowed red as if he had been branded by Our Lord so that all might know to what purpose his life had been committed and why he was to be brought by good men to such a deserved end.'

Marlow's description of the scene as the seer was dragged along to the place of execution went on for pages. McBaith skipped large sections. It occurred to him from the detailed description of the site of the execution that it had taken place just where Macpherson's workshop had stood before Ally Taggart had set it on fire. The seer and his wife had been tied to two stakes and then branches had been piled around them 'up to the height of his huge and powerful chest'. Then the villagers had thrown their torches into the branches and 'tall flames and the terrible screams of the seer's wife told a tale to the night'.

'The seer spoke in a loud voice to the end, shouting above the yelling of the mob, and the last thing he did say was "I pledge a covenant with you, folk of Aragarr. When seventy-seven-thousand-seven-hundred-and-seventy-seven days are gone then will I return and wreak my vengeance and wash my hands in the blood of Aragarr. Remember the magic seven for I will come again when one of my blood returns from far away. He will be the seventh son of a seventh son and will fulfil his destiny".'

Janet looked at McBaith and in answer to the question in her eyes he gave a brief nod.

'I'm a seventh son of a seventh son,' he said quietly. He and Janet sat in silence watching MacLean as the writer took a calculator from a drawer and began to prod at it with his finger, muttering to himself as he carried out his calculations.

His eyes were wide when he had finished. He looked from one to the other without speaking for a moment then said: 'I'd have to double check to be sure but ... '

'Just tell us,' McBaith almost yelled.

'Today,' MacLean said.

McBaith stood up quickly and shook hands with MacLean. 'You've been a great help. Thanks for everything.'

'But ... '

'We've got to get back to Aragarr.'

Janet gulped the last of her tea and followed him out the door.

'Maybe I'm meant to be some kind of witness to what's going to happen,' he said to Janet as he sent the car shooting back along the road to Aragarr.

'What is going to happen?'

'Who knows ... but I've seen enough to know it's going to be kind of ugly. We both know this is all crazy ... but it's happening ... '

'I'm scared.'

'Me too.'

'Maybe we shouldn't go back,' she said.

He scuffed his foot lightly over the brake.

'I've got to go back. But you're right ... I should have thought of it myself ... there's no reason why you shouldn't stay in Aultglen.'

'No ... '

'Yeah, why should I ... '

'No,' she said, determinedly, 'if you go, I go.'
'But ... '
'Just drive,' she said. 'You're right ... we do have to go back.'

He drove slowly for another mile, trying to talk her out of coming back with him, but she had made up her mind. He had mixed feelings about that – if she stayed behind she might be safer, but if she was with him at least he would be there if something dangerous did happen.

When he was certain she wouldn't have a change of heart he accelerated, sending the car screaming along the road, gobbling up the miles.

He felt the change in atmosphere at precisely the same point he had noticed it when he had been leaving Aragarr – about a mile north of the village, at a bend where a tall birch stretched a branch out over the road like a reaching arm.

But it seemed more than just a before-the-storm heaviness now. It was like stepping from torrential rain into a crypt which was loaded not only with the sluggish, crushed-air, hard-to-breathe feeling of outside but also with a terrible gloom and a sense of unknowable threat.

An ugly sensation of apprehension and melancholy began to seep into him and he felt suddenly tired and depressed. It was as if he had been injected with something indescribably vile.

It was as he slowed to turn off the main road and head down the hill into Aragarr that he felt the wheel stiffen in his hands. At first he thought the car had been hit by a sudden gust of wind but that idea disappeared when the wheel began to jerk about violently, wrenching the car from side to side.

Janet screamed. 'What are you doing?'
'It's not me,' he yelled. 'Something's pulling the wheel.'

The rational side of his brain tried to pretend it might be some steering fault, some nut that had come loose, a section of fatigued metal which had broken. But he knew it wasn't anything like that.

It was as if another pair of hands were on the wheel, tugging at it.

As they shot past the turn-off, he felt the car lift onto two wheels. Concentrating all his strength he managed to snap the steering-wheel to the left. The car banged back onto its four wheels with a thudding, scraping sound.

He kicked at the brake and when the car's speed eased he snatched on the handbrake, pulling it all the way up and locking it there.

The car slewed violently to the left and he swung with it, steering into the skid, fighting for control as they shot towards a drainage ditch.

'Hold on,' he yelled the instant before the car's two left-hand wheels gouged parallel trenches along the muddy roadside and disappeared over the edge of the ditch.

A sheet of water geysered up from the ditch as the car plunged into it and an instant later there was a loud metallic crunch and the patter of glass showering across metal as the far bank of the ditch punched into the car's side doors. The car trembled, its engine coughing for a moment, then lay still, like a dead thing.

McBaith swung around and grabbed for Janet. Her eyes were dazed, shocked, but he couldn't see any injuries and a surge of relief passed through him.

'I'm ... all right,' she said. 'I think I am anyway.' She gave him a shaky grin.

'Looks like we go the rest of the way on foot,' he muttered, shoving open his door and cursing himself for not insisting she remain in Aultglen.

He helped her out of the car, holding her under the arms and lifting her over the ditch. Then they started down the hill at a half run.

When approaching Aragarr harbour from the north in his trawler the *Aragarr Lass*, Murdo Melrose always made sure he gave the reef west of the harbour a wide berth. He had known since he was a boy that it wasn't the rocks you could see peeping up through the white water that you had to be wary of – it was those you couldn't see, a few feet under the surface. Like all good skippers, he put safety first and always treated the sea and all its dangers with a healthy respect.

This day was no exception.

He had planned to give the reef as wide a berth as he ever had ...

... yet now he was suddenly aware that the Aragarr Lass *was heading straight for the reef.*

Aware that for the last five minutes he had been in some kind of a dream.

He realised that he couldn't remember anything about that period. They had rounded the end of the bay and he had struck a course with his eye ...

Then *nothing*.

Now the bow of the boat was ploughing its way in a line that would take them right onto the foam-covered rocks only two hundred yards away. His brow furrowed as he swung the wheel to starboard but felt no shift in the boat's course.

That was when his younger brother appeared in the wheelhouse.

'What are you doing, Murdo?' David Melrose said and Murdo noted the alarm in his voice.

'I ... it's not responding.'

He swung the wheel to starboard again but again there was no response.

One hundred yards.

Ninety.

Eighty.

He tried to cut the engines, tried to swing to the port side and skirt the rocks to the left.

But nothing responded now.

Fifty yards.

It was as if the running of the boat had been taken out of his hands.

It had to be a nightmare.

Thirty yards.

'I don't believe what's happening,' he yelled as his brother grabbed for the wheel.

Then the boat hit – huge, jagged rocks snarling through the bow section.

The men were thrown violently forward as the boat climbed onto the rocks, its timbers shrieking.

Murdo was the first to his feet, wiping blood from a gash in his forehead with his sleeve.

'Get the men into the lifeboat,' he yelled, dragging his brother to his feet.

Water was gushing through a great hole in the deck now and huge waves were washing over the side.

It was as he ran from the wheelhouse that he realised the sky had filled with black stormclouds.

But how? The sky had been relatively clear when they had entered the bay.

How was it possible?

How was any of this possible?

Sixteen

It took McBaith and Janet only a few minutes to get down the hill but in that time the sky seemed to fill with ugly, black clouds that came scudding over the horizon. As they passed the school and entered the village McBaith noticed an unnatural stillness in the air and an eerie silence about the place.

The calm before the storm.

The words popped into his head and hung there.

At first the village appeared to be deserted and McBaith thought: *Too late. It's happened already.* As they turned into the High Street he began unconsciously to dissect the words. Too late for what? What had happened already?

They found a crowd of people gathered at the Jacobite Arms, crammed into both bars and spilling into the street.

Malcolm saw them coming and hurried to meet them.

'They went up to Meg's,' he said. 'Andrews and Macpherson and some of the others. I tried to stop them but ... '

'What did they do?'

'She wasn't there ... I'm sure they'd have killed her if she had been. They've left a man up there to wait for her and other groups are searching for her.'

Macpherson appeared at Malcolm's side. 'Well, did you find out anything?'

McBaith nodded.

'What?' Macpherson said then added quickly: 'No, it concerns us all, you'd better come inside and tell everybody.'

Macpherson forced a way through the crowd and McBaith followed, holding Janet's hand as if he feared he might lose her if he let go.

Inside the Jacobite Arms everyone seemed to be talking at once and Macpherson had to yell above the din to get everyone's attention.

'Quiet. Be quiet. Listen.'

Instantly a hush fell over the crowd and every face turned to look at Macpherson.

'Al McBaith has something to say about all this,' Macpherson said. 'I suggest that we all listen.'

As McBaith outlined what he and Janet had discovered, he noticed the number of guns in the crowd – he counted at least ten shotguns and half a dozen rifles.

A lynch mob, a voice in his head said. That was what they were. They intended to kill Meg and nothing was going to stop them.

When he had finished speaking, silence hung in the air for a moment, then Jack Andrews shouted from the back of the room: 'That settles any arguments, doesn't it? Annie said Meg had to die to stop all this. We have to find her and kill her.'

'I'm still for calling the police,' another voice said from the edge of the crowd.

'Aye, let the police handle it,' agreed a woman's voice.

'I agree with Jack,' Macpherson said and a grumble of approval filled the room.

'If we can lay our hands on her,' Neil Ritchie shouted, 'we have no choice but to lift the curse by killing her. That's just what it is, a curse.'

'Now hold on just a minute,' McBaith said, holding his hands in the air. 'Let's think about this before we do something we might all regret. We can't just go out there and kill her. At least we want some answers first, at least we should talk to her.' Why was he standing up for her? Crazy as the truth was, it was *the truth*. How could he have any doubts now? What else could they do but kill her? Wouldn't that stop what was going on? Annie Stewart had said it would. Without the communicant, evil could not prevail – that was what the old woman had said.

So why did he feel he had to try to save Meg? Was he just grabbing for the rational, reacting in the way he had been trained to, attempting to find a sane way out of a situation which really offered no such exit?

Or maybe it was his destiny?

Destiny.

Maybe.

Maybe he was meant to talk for her, to argue her case.

Destiny. An irritated voice in his head yelled the word.

Why was he thinking such things? To hell with destiny. They were all in danger and his brain was still trying to normalise things which made no sense at all.

'This isn't your village,' Andrews was shouting. 'I told you that before and ... '

His sentence remained half-finished, hanging in the air, as a small, plump man barged into the room, his face red with exertion.

'There's a boat ... on the ... reef,' he panted. 'Someone ... better call ... the Coastguard or ... '

As he continued talking, puffing out his story, several men rushed from the pub.

Macpherson grabbed for the telephone and snatched a coin from his pocket. He fiddled with the receiver cradle, dialled, then hung up and threw a glance at McBaith.

'I think the phone's out,' he said, picking up the receiver and trying again.

After a moment, he handed the receiver to McBaith.

'It's dead,' he said but his words conveyed more than just a simple statement about a malfunctioning telephone.

As a tall, red-haired woman near the door shouted, 'I'll call them from my house' and rushed out, McBaith took the receiver and listened.

What he heard was a silence beyond silence, the nothingness of still air in a deep cave.

He handed the receiver back to Macpherson without a word and felt Janet's hand gripping his arm. He looked down into her eyes and saw the questions there.

He shook his head slowly. 'I think we're cut off. I think Aragarr is cut off ... from everything.'

The red-haired woman returned a moment later and looked quizzically around the faces in the crowd.

'My phone's out too,' she said, 'and Sandy Ross tried the public box on the corner and it's broken as well.'

'Well,' Macpherson sighed, 'I suppose we'd all better see if we can help with the boat.'

McBaith and Janet followed in the wake of the crowd as they filed out of the pub into the street.

Outside, it was as if night was about to fall. The black clouds filled the sky now, shutting out almost all of the sunlight. The air was heavy and cold.

As they hurried along the harbour towards the sea-wall, thunder exploded in the sky, a distant rumbling at first, like an artillery barrage ripping along a far-away hillside, then single blasts that seemed as if they would split open the heavens. Rain began to teem down, lashing off the street.

'They're all right,' somebody shouted just as McBaith reached the sea-wall, 'they're in the lifeboat.'

A jagged shaft of white lightning quivered through the darkness and McBaith caught a glimpse of a small boat bobbing in huge waves, making for the beach several hundred yards north of the harbour. Figures on the beach were shouting to the men in the boat.

He jerked his head around as a car screamed up the High Street and skidded to a halt. Jack Andrews sprinted to the car and he heard the driver shout: 'She's back. Meg Rees. She's up at her cottage. I've left Peter there to make sure she doesn't get away.'

'Did she see you?'

'No.'

'What is she doing?'

'Just sitting at her window ... she's not doing anything. I ...'

'Good. Now's the time to finish this.'

Andrews climbed into the car and it reversed up the street. Other people were running for their cars now and McBaith saw two men loading shotguns in the back of a Ford as it shot past.

No sense.

Didn't make any sense at all.

But they had to do it, didn't they?

There couldn't be any doubts left in his mind now.

It was crazy but it was real.

McBaith had the sudden feeling he was hallucinating, that the last week of his life had never really taken place. What had happened to that distant country when life had been flesh and bone and concrete and cars and grass and trees? Where was that small island he had lived on where all the pieces of the jigsaw fitted, where there were no real unknowns?

He found himself facing Macpherson.

'Have you got your car here?'

Macpherson nodded.

'Let's go then.'

As they hurried through the rain, McBaith saw that Malcolm was alongside him.

'Malcolm, will you take Janet back to the hotel? I ... '

'No, I'm coming,' the older man shouted above a clap of thunder.

'But ... '

'I'm going with you too,' Janet said. 'I'm not staying here.'

There was no more time to argue. They had reached the car. As McBaith got into the back seat, he saw a rifle on the floor in the front. Malcolm picked it up without saying a word and held it across his chest.

The world had gone mad. Swinton MacLean's words were spinning through his head. *Meggy was a girl of innocence ... corrupted by the seer ... used as a sacrifice in some devilish ritual ...*

Images of the Aragarr Seer's last moments were there too, as if they were unfolding in front of his eyes.

Then the seer's words, screamed through the flames, ravaged across McBaith's mind.

I pledge a covenant with you ... wash my hands in the blood of Aragarr ... I will come again ...

Come again. Come again.

Annie's words too, whispered to him.

There is a communicant here, drawing in the evil. Trying to destroy the village. Communicant must die.

Macpherson accelerated hard and the car shot along the

street. No one spoke now, the only sound was the damp flick-flack as the windscreen wipers desperately tried to keep back the flood of water blurring Macpherson's view.

The sun had appeared again, McBaith saw. It was peeping between two black clouds, dribbling out weak, watery light which bathed the village in a smoky, ghostly pall.

Suddenly Macpherson braked violently and the car slewed along the street. McBaith grabbed for Janet as she was flung forward and managed to drag her to him as the car bumped up onto the kerb and shuddered to a halt.

'What the hell ... ' McBaith yelled.

Then his eyes followed Janet's and he saw the great rip across the road ...

It was about a foot wide, a rent in the earth which started at the harbour front, sliced through solid stone, then ran fifteen feet across the street.

And it was moving, lengthening, gouging a slow trail through the tar, heading straight for a two-storey house.

'We'll never get past,' Macpherson mumbled.

'There must be another way,' McBaith bawled. 'There has to be.'

'Go up the lane,' Malcolm said to Macpherson.

'Yes ... yes, you're right ... the lane ... '

Get Meg. Kill Meg. Kill the evil. They were right of course.

The point of the trench seemed to hesitate in front of the house and quiver there. Then each bank began to move, widening the black hole to three feet ...

Six feet.

Ten feet.

It was a yawning ravine now, sending scores of long trembling slits shooting across the road.

As Macpherson wrenched the car into reverse and sent it roaring backwards, McBaith saw the point of the expanding trench leap forward and punch into the house. A single brick fell first, then the entire upper storey folded forward and thundered into the street in a cloud of plaster dust.

'What is it?' Malcolm said dully.

McBaith shook his head jerkily, unable to answer. The skin of his face felt like quick-drying cement.

Another ditch was slicing along the centre of the High Street now, its ragged edges widening. A tributary shot out of it and bit into the foundations of a small whitewashed cottage. A wall collapsed and the roof swayed, hung there for a moment, then came apart and crashed down.

The car shot into a narrow lane, bouncing and swaying on old cobbles.

'Like an earthquake ... ' Janet muttered several times, to no-one in particular.

No doubt, a voice said in McBaith's head. No doubt now. No doubt about anything.

Macpherson swung the car right and they were on a track, muddy water splashing up the sides of the car.

As they reached the road that climbed the hill and Macpherson jerked the car onto it, Malcolm pointed back at the village, his eyes wide.

A dozen great ditches were snaking through Aragarr now, expanding trenches that devoured houses and entire gardens, swallowed lanes and birch trees, gnawed away large sections of the High Street.

Janet buried her face in McBaith's chest and he held her. Squinting to see through the torrential rain which pounded at the back window, he glimpsed mountainous waves thundering into the harbour. The two houses nearest him collapsed simultaneously, bricks, furniture and wooden beams tumbling into the street, then in one petrified second a cottage just outside the village disappeared as if gulped down into the bowels of the earth.

Then he saw something else.

Dim shapes ...

(animals?)

... moving out of the trees and darting between the houses. The rear window was getting misted up and he rubbed at it with his hand.

Yes, animals.

Dozens of animals padding along the High Street, trotting into the gardens, thin shadows in the lanes and tracks.

He saw two shapes about the size of small dogs leap at a woman and watched as she tried to fight them off then was pulled down out of sight.

His eyes shifted and he picked out a larger form leaping through the air at the side of a house. A window smashed and the curtains bucked as the animal plunged inside.

Nightmare.
Lunatic asylum.
Not really happening.

'Got to kill her,' Malcolm was saying now and McBaith looked around and saw that Malcolm too had seen the animals invade the village.

Yes.
Of course.
Had to kill her now.
She was communicant, drawing in evil.
Kill her and it would stop.
The nightmare would go away.
But kill ...
Couldn't just kill people.

The rational part of him demanded to be heard. Even now. It had ruled him for so long, like a bad drinking habit. But what place did it have here, among all this?

'There's Andrews and the others,' Macpherson said and McBaith peered out the front window and saw the rear lights of several cars through the slanting rain.

Brake lights began to wink and he realised the cars were turning into the track to Meg Rees's house.

'We can't just kill her,' he heard himself say.

'Don't try to stop us, Al,' Macpherson said and there was a cold anger in his voice.

'It has to be done,' Malcolm said dully, like someone reading the words of an obscure ritual.

They swung along the track, drawing close to the car in front.

McBaith saw the house and it seemed as if all the lights were on, greyish pools of light glowing all round the garden.

A pair of red brake-lights flashed, parallel scarlet lines ripping through the darkness. An instant later McBaith heard the muffled sound of a car door being slammed, a voice yelling in anger and the brutal thud of a shotgun.

Seventeen

As Macpherson's car bumped to a halt in the long grass in front of the low fence which surrounded Meg Rees's house, McBaith saw men tumbling out of cars all around him. Beyond them he saw the first car to draw up with its door yawning open. Beside that car, in the glow of the interior lights, two men were struggling with small dim shapes. One man had a shotgun broken open in his right hand and seemed to be trying to slot cartridges into the gun as one of the shapes bit at his arm. The second man – who McBaith thought was Jack Andrews – was on the ground struggling with several dark forms.

Dogs?

They looked like dogs.

But they had bushy tails and ...

He saw they were foxes as he jumped out of the car.

Foxes.

A dozen or more, jumping at the men, their teeth biting and slashing.

A rifle roared once, twice, three times and three of the shapes were kicked back into the blackness.

The man with the open shotgun was wielding it like a club now, shrieking as his flesh was ripped open.

Several men were dragging the foxes from the man on the ground.

Did foxes do this?

McBaith was sure they didn't.

They attacked chickens. Things like that. *Not men.*

The gun barked again and other guns joined in until the clearing around the house was filled with the continuous bam of weapons and the acrid smell of gunsmoke.

He saw the man on the ground being pulled to his feet, his clothes covered in blood. It was Andrews.

He heard him shout: 'Get me my shotgun.'

Janet grabbed for McBaith's arm as she got out of the car. He turned to her and was about to say 'Stay in the car' when it came to him like a sudden pain that if he had had his way Janet would still be in the village.

That village of horror.

No. She would not stay in the car. She would go with him wherever he went, never out of his sight.

'Stay close to me,' he said to her.

As he turned back to the men, he caught a glimpse of a white shape hurrying through the darkness at the back of the house. His eyes passed over it but he looked again quickly and as it disappeared into the trees he was sure he saw Meg Rees, her face turned towards them, looking back over her shoulder.

'There she is,' a voice shouted and he saw Macpherson swing around and bring up his rifle.

His shoulder jerked with the kick of the weapon and McBaith heard the bullet whipping through the trees.

'You can't just shoot her,' he heard himself shout.

Why?

Why did he still insist on holding back from total belief in all the evidence?

Why did he still want to grab for a civilised answer when there wasn't one?

These men were right. She had to *die*.

Macpherson fired again and McBaith saw the branch of a tree explode.

Then two men jumped the fence, shotguns held over their chests, and began to run towards the point where Meg had disappeared.

The firing in the clearing had ceased now and McBaith saw that all the foxes were dead. Andrews was covered in blood but had managed to get his hands on his shotgun and was leading a group of several men towards the fence. The bolt on Macpherson's rifle gave a sharp snick as he flicked another bullet into the chamber and followed.

McBaith looked from Malcolm to Janet, then said, 'C'mon,' grabbed her hand and started after the men.

A moment later they were in the trees, jogging along a path. McBaith looked back from time to time to make sure Malcolm was keeping up.

It was like neither night nor day in the forest. The light that bled down through the branches was unlike both sunlight and moonlight – it was like a weakly-glowing white mist.

The rain stopped suddenly but the forest on either side of them remained alive with the sound of dripping water plopping from sodden branches.

'Stay together,' McBaith heard a voice shout up ahead of him. 'Don't get separated. She can't be far ahead of us.' The words seemed heavy, as if they were being swallowed up by invisible moisture oozing from the forest.

Then they burst into a clearing. McBaith saw immediately that there were several paths leading out of it. But which one had Meg taken?

A man shouted 'Here' and held up a tiny piece of white material which he had taken from the sharp point of a branch. 'This way.'

The man had taken two steps along the narrow path when he froze. The others hesitated, peering beyond him.

Twenty yards along the path McBaith could make out a huge stag, its head held low, one of its hooves digging angrily at the ground. It looked somehow unreal in the strange light which seemed to make it shine luminously.

For a moment nobody moved. It was as if they had all been turned to stone. McBaith felt as if the only moving thing in the whole world was the stag's leg, jerking as it stabbed its hoof into the ground again and again.

Then the stag raised its head and the pale light accentuated its magnificent antlers.

As it charged, Macpherson fired and a chunk of its antlers exploded, scattering white fragments through the air.

The man on the path fired the first barrel of his shotgun wildly into the forest, tried to run for it, then turned back and fired again at point-blank range the instant before the antlers bit into his chest and hooked him high into the air.

The stag was among the men now, snorting furiously and hooking its antlers at the darting figures. Puffs of white breath shot from its nostrils. McBaith saw that the shotgun blast had taken away one eye.

A tall figure tried to hold his ground and get in a shot but a vicious flick of the antlers cut him down. Another man was sent flying into the low branches of a tree as he tried to run for it.

Shotguns roared and blood spurted from the stag's body but it was Macpherson's second shot which made it freeze in its tracks.

It watched them with glazed eyes for a moment then its hind legs collapsed and it fell and lay still.

A plump man with a rifle was first along the path and the rest of them followed.

'We've got to get her, Al,' McBaith heard Malcolm saying and saw the old man hurrying along beside him. 'We've got to kill Meg ... to stop all this. This just doesn't happen ... '

'Save your breath,' McBaith said, then added: 'If you can't keep up we'll fall out and rest for a couple of minutes.'

'No ... can't stop ... not now ... '

They plunged on as the path narrowed, branches from both sides mingling above their heads.

McBaith heard a voice up ahead shouting, 'There she is,' and the hollow bam of a shotgun.

'They've seen her,' he said to Janet, tightening his grip on her hand and glancing briefly back at her.

His eyes just brushed across her.

But for that instant it was Janet ... *yet not Janet!*

It was her but she was dressed in a long black robe, her hair hanging free, unstyled.

He looked again quickly and it was *his* Janet now.

He was seeing things again. But what did it mean this time?

Was there something terrible in store for her? Did she have some destiny part to play in all this too?

Why had he seen her dressed like that?

Had some distant ancestor of hers yelled her hate of the seer into his face as the flames consumed him?

Was everyone in Aragarr being led along by the nose to some hideous end in retribution for what had been done?

The sins of the fathers, McBaith thought. But what had the sins of their ancestors been? They had killed an evil man, The Black Seer of Aragarr, some kind of black magician. He had deserved it if anyone had.

If there was one thing in my life I could change right now, he thought, it would be that I had managed to talk Janet into staying in Aultglen.

The sound of another gunshot snatched away his thoughts. Up ahead, beyond the bobbing shoulders of the men, he caught a brief glimpse of a flash of white.

A dress?

It had to be Meg Rees.

At that moment, he wanted her dead more than any of them.

'She can't get away now,' someone shouted.

'She's out of sight,' another voice yelled.

'Yes, but she's just gone around that bend.'

They swept around the bend in the path and McBaith saw the flash of white again as Meg crossed a dark clearing. Two guns boomed but she was gone again, out of sight.

'What if ... guns don't ... kill her,' Malcolm puffed but McBaith ignored the question.

If guns didn't kill her, they were all dead.

The men at the front rushed into the clearing and it was at that moment that McBaith realised the clearing was moving.

It was alive.

Eighteen

McBaith stared into the clearing.

It was shifting, writhing, a dark mass of subtle movement.

Suddenly the clouds and trees seemed to part and a shaft of trembling, watery light fell across the clearing.

It was covered in animals.

Weasels, wildcats, foxes, stoats, mink ...

Scores of them, McBaith thought, then corrected himself.

Hundreds.

For one frozen moment they didn't attack, just watched the men.

McBaith drew Janet back as she peered in horror into the clearing. Then five mink leapt at the first man, their teeth flashing. His shotgun roared and the sound was followed immediately by an outburst of gunfire. McBaith saw the first man fall and the second struggling with brown shapes which leapt on him. He spun away, pushing Malcolm and dragging Janet, as the entire clearing seemed to shift like a groundsheet being dragged quickly across the grass.

As they ran back along the path he was aware of the thud of feet behind them as some of the men followed. Beyond them he could hear gunfire and screams and yelping, squalling and snarling.

He hadn't gone more than a hundred yards when he stopped.

There was no point in running, no point in doing anything unless they killed Meg Rees.

The thought scorched into his mind and hung there.

While she lived the horror would go on.

While she lived they would never leave the forest alive.

While she lived the destruction of Aragarr would continue.

Macpherson was right behind him and he grabbed the big man by the arm.

'There's nothing we can do for those men back there ... or for the village ... unless we can get to Meg,' he yelled.

Macpherson looked at him as if he was a stranger, his eyes wild.

'You're right,' Andrews yelled, running up to them.

'Is there a way around the clearing?' McBaith said.

'Through the trees. Yes.'

Andrews shook Macpherson and the big man seemed to suddenly realise where he was, who they were.

'You all right?' McBaith said.

'Aye, I'll be fine.' His eyes remained glazed, confused.

'The mink were eating Charlie Macfarlane's face,' he said in a hollow voice, 'and there were stoats on ... '

Andrews interrupted. 'Come on,' he said and ducked into the trees.

McBaith looked back along the path before he followed but none of the other men were in sight.

Andrews set a fast pace, bent double under the lower branches of the trees and half jogging through the dimness. He seemed to know exactly where he was going. McBaith brought up the rear, keeping the five of them together. 'Left,' Andrews said waving a hand through the air, then a moment later he said 'Left' again.

The gunfire was distant now, more sporadic. McBaith found his mind conjuring up terrible pictures of what was happening in that clearing.

Had any of the other men managed to get away? Or climb a tree. Or fight the animals off? Or were they all ...

Being eaten alive.

He shook his head, casting the thoughts aside.

All around them the foliage seemed to be breathing softly, expanding after the hammering rain had compressed it down.

'Here it is,' Andrews said and McBaith saw they were on a path again. It was very narrow with barely room for his shoulders to fit between the trees and overgrown with long wet grass.

'She won't get away,' Andrews said, a kind of exhilaration and sense of anticipated triumph edging aside the fear in his voice. 'This path doesn't lead anywhere.'

'That's right,' Malcolm said. 'It comes out at the clifftops.'

As they ran on, McBaith caught the briefest glimpse of the man away to his left – a face framed between two branches, watching him. There for an instant then gone.

That face.

With the bloodshot eyes and the great scar on the forehead and the putrid hanging flesh.

The man had seemed to be smiling at him, reassuring him that everything would be all right, beckoning him to come into the trees.

The panting in McBaith's chest seemed to ease. His shoulders relaxed.

Everything would be all right, wouldn't it?

Of course it would.

Because everything was happening as it was *meant to*.

McBaith looked up ahead of him, over Andrews' shoulders, at a shimmering beam of weak light ...

... and it looked so warm ...

... so beautiful.

It began to divide into tiny fragments, each one a thing of such intense beauty that it almost hurt to look at it.

Why did people see things as having a oneness when there were really millions of parts ...

'What's wrong,' Janet gasped.

'Wrong?' He looked down at her.

'Yes. You were ... smiling.'

'No. No, I wasn't.'

Andrews yelled, 'There she is' and Macpherson fired in the same instant, the bullet hitting a tree with a dull thunk.

McBaith saw the white dress billowing out as Meg ran, her long fair hair flying out behind her.

And she seemed to be bathed in *light*.

That exquisite light.

It was just that she was wearing a white dress, he told himself. That was all it was, an optical illusion.

But no ...

How could they be thinking of killing a thing of such beauty?

Meg ran into a broad, uneven clearing strewn with huge boulders. McBaith saw that it ended abruptly two hundred yards away in a line of jagged rocks and that beyond them, far below, the dark back of the sea moved restlessly.

Here was the place of the sacrifice, a voice in his head said. *Why? What did that mean?*

Meg darted behind one of the boulders as Macpherson fired again. The bullet ricocheted off stone with a loud, ugly whine.

'We've got her now,' Andrews yelled, sprinting forward.

Meg appeared again and McBaith heard her scream, 'No, doooon't' and her words scraped painfully through him.

And she was bathed in light, encapsulated in that light of a thousand fragments.

Like diamonds.

Andrews raised his shotgun but before he could fire there was a heavy flapping sound and a shape about six feet across seemed to come from nowhere and drop over him, clawing and biting.

McBaith could make out jerking wings and a flashing beak.

'An eagle,' Janet screamed, her voice sharp and harsh, with the texture of shattering glass. 'It's a golden eagle.'

The shotgun roared as Andrews flailed the gun desperately around his head in an effort to fight the bird off. Fire lanced out of the barrel and the buckshot sprayed into the high branches.

McBaith made no move to help. He felt strangely detached.

He gazed at Meg and saw she was standing with her back to the jagged rocks at the top of the cliffs now. Beyond her was nothing but a long, long drop.

She was staring at him and he could see the light around

her was expanding now, growing larger and larger, more and more beautiful ...

... *and it seemed to be speaking to him.*

Words spat into his mind as clearly as if they were being spoken into his ear.

'*I pledge a covenant with you, folk of Aragarr* ... '

Andrews screamed but the sound seemed to come from far away.

'*When seventy-seven-thousand-seven-hundred-and-seventy-seven days are gone then will I return* ... '

Macpherson raised his rifle and McBaith saw now that Meg was laughing, giggling like a girl. It was as if she was oblivious to the danger.

'*Wash my hands in the blood of Aragarr.*'

McBaith felt so drowsy, so ...

Not giggling like a little girl. *Cackling like an evil old witch.*

Why had he seen innocence when ...

Macpherson's finger tightened on the trigger.

'*One of my blood will return from far away* ... *Seventh son of a seventh son* ... '

The barrel of Macpherson's rifle was knocked upwards as if by an invisible fist. The rifle kicked and the bullet snarled skywards. The big man tried to hold onto his rifle but something fought with him, trying to pull it away, ripping at his jacket, an invisible hand grabbing at his face, twisting his mouth, flattening his nose.

So drowsy. He could sleep forever.

In that light.

It seemed as if it filled half the clearing now, with Meg at its centre, a million fragments of eternal delight.

'Do something Al,' a voice yelled.

He looked at Malcolm and saw that the old man had fallen down and something was tearing at him, a blurred shape. Not an animal. Not a bird. Just a dim blurred outline of something ...

Not of this world.

Not real.

'Meggy ...'

He stared into the light, felt as if he was about to be swallowed up by it.

'*Meggy, he's here to fulfil his destiny.*'

Destiny?

How could he think of killing poor Meggy?

She who was sacrificed ...

Macpherson's rifle was jerked out of his hands and he swung his fist through the air at the invisible thing ...

Not invisible.

McBaith could see something between himself and Macpherson now. Like an outline of something that had no substance.

No existence on this earth?

Macpherson fell over and wrestled about on the ground. Andrews screamed, still flailing his shotgun about his head, jabbing at the beak which snapped at him, swinging for the powerful flapping wings.

Destiny?

Yes, destiny.

The Time of the Six.

SIX.

Why did he keep thinking of numbers?

What significance did they have?

What did *six* have to do with anything?

'Aaaaaaal.'

Janet's voice.

He turned slowly, like a man on heavy tranquillisers.

Janet was on the ground too, far away, near the treeline. It was as if she had been lifted up and flung there.

Had to stop being drowsy.

Had to.

Kill Meg.

Couldn't kill Meg.

Not beautiful Meggy.

Not while she was in the light.

The light that was still expanding, still fragmenting into more exquisite pieces.

Not his destiny to kill poor Meggy. That was laughable.

His mind was a whirlpool of thoughts and strange words, inhibiting action, drowning his instincts.

'*The Seer of Aragarr has returned to wash his hands in blood ... Seventh son of a ...*'

'Aaaaal.'

Had to kill Meg.

Destiny. Crap.

He eyes picked out Macpherson's rifle and he took a step towards it.

His legs were heavy, awkward.

Do it, a voice yelled in his head. Make your will dominate the words in your head.

Do it.

Clammy, rotten hands grabbed his shoulders, pulling him back. A putrid smell wafted up his nostrils. He had a feeling of drowning in filth.

Never get to the rifle.

Would.

Dammit, he would.

The hands grabbed at his face now and he flung out his elbows. He made contact with something but he wasn't sure what it was. It did not have the substance of something real, yet it was not air. It was like a piece of incredibly light fabric.

But the hands were so strong, twisting his head round. And he was tired and weak ...

And the light.

And poor Meggy.

He was on his knees now.

The hell with Meg.

Had to die.

Kill her.

So drowsy.

Nooooooo.

He summoned all his strength, kicked himself up and dived for Macpherson's rifle. Fingernails raked across his face. Hands dragged at his ankles, tugged at his hair.

Kill her.

He brought up the rifle but something jerked the barrel away.

The light was still expanding, filling the clearing now.

So beautiful.

Dammit.

He snapped the rifle back and fired.

The bullet punched into Meg Rees, almost cutting her in half. He saw a gush of blood against her white dress as she flew backwards, hit the jagged stones, rolled over and lay still.

The strange light disappeared instantly.

Had it ever really been there?

He felt the grasping fingers move from his body, heard the flap of the eagle's wings as it flew back towards the trees, was aware of a sudden stillness all around him.

He rolled onto his back and felt warm sunlight on his face. The black clouds were moving fast now, as if before a strong wind, and in the distance he could see a clear sky.

There was no drowsiness now, no alien words in his mind, no light that talked to him.

He didn't want to ask questions because he knew there could be no answers.

Suddenly Janet was holding his face and he smiled up at her.

'Are you all right?' she said.

'Just great.'

He looked around him. Malcolm was sitting nearby, rubbing his face. Macpherson had stood up and was staring at McBaith, a thousand questions in his eyes.

McBaith shrugged and jumped to his feet, his arm around Janet's shoulders.

'Where is she?'

It was Andrews' voice, high-pitched, almost shrill.

McBaith turned and saw the blood-stained figure of Andrews striding about the rocks at the clifftop.

'In the name of God, where is she?'

McBaith hurried to the spot where Meg had fallen but there was no sign of her. He searched the grass and the rocks but there was no body, not a trace of blood, not a scrap of evidence to show she had ever been there.

'She went over the cliff,' Macpherson said.

McBaith looked at him. 'Did she?'

'There can't be any other answer.'

McBaith knew what he meant. They were back in the rational world. Everything that had happened had to be normalised or forgotten.

They walked back along the path in silence. Sunshine bled through the branches of the trees now and McBaith saw the black clouds were withdrawing, scudding away towards the horizon.

A few minutes later, they met Neil Ritchie. There was blood on the sleeve of his jacket and he had a shotgun in his hand.

He looked at Janet and said: 'Thank God you're all right.'

'What happened ... at the clearing?' Macpherson said.

'A lot were killed,' Ritchie said in a frayed, exhausted voice. 'The animals were ... just like mad things. Then suddenly ... they just stopped and went back into the forest ... as if it had all been a big mistake.' He shifted his red, haunted eyes to McBaith: 'It's over, isn't it? One of you killed her.'

McBaith nodded. 'It's over.'

It was as he slipped his hand over Janet's shoulders and started to walk again that the word came to him.

Like the far-away cry of a sea-bird reaching him across a silent sea shrouded in drifting, early-morning mist, on the very outer limits of his hearing.

Six.

He didn't have to ask; he knew he was the only one who had heard it.

Nineteen

'Penny for your thoughts,' Janet said strolling through the French windows from the sunny balcony.

She looked more beautiful than ever, he thought. Two weeks in Spain had done her good. She was wearing a tiny white bikini, the one which was so small she would never wear to the beach but didn't mind wearing around their villa when only he was there. Her fair skin, which had turned a light pink on the first week of their honeymoon, was beginning to switch to a soft brown.

'I was just thinking about ... you know.'

'What?'

'Aragarr.'

'Again! What about it this time?' she said and he thought he detected a mild reprimand in her voice.

'About everything that happened.'

She lowered herself onto his knee and he put down the book he had been reading.

'Has the book helped you ... to understand?'

He glanced at it. *The Possibilities* it was called, a kind of encyclopedia of paranormal events.

'A little. One question keeps hanging in my mind.'

'What?'

'If I hadn't shot Meg Rees, would there have been anything left of Aragarr?'

She shrugged and kissed him lightly on the lips. 'Who knows. Things are bad enough as they are ... twenty people dead, most of the village in ruins. It's a miracle there's *anything* left of it ... thank God Malcolm's hotel escaped ... '

'Yeah, I know. But if we hadn't got to Meg ... would the village have just ... gone down a hole or something?'

'We'll never know.'

They had left Aragarr two days after the day of the horror, after answering seemingly endless questions from the police, and had had a three-week holiday in London, staying in a rented flat in Bloomsbury. Then one morning he had woken up and said: 'Let's get married.' They were so right together he knew it was the thing he wanted most in the world. He had sent a plane ticket to Malcolm and the old man had been their best man at the registry office wedding. He and Janet had caught a plane to Spain the next day. They had had an idyllic two weeks in their villa, which stood alone on a hillside above a beach and had a vast balcony and its own swimming-pool.

But the memories didn't fade. Questions remained, plaguing him like scores of little demons. Questions about numbers and feelings of fear and destiny. The strangest thing of all, he told Janet and Malcolm, was that the sense of impending danger and of being trapped by destiny, being led, were still with him, undiminished.

Malcolm told him that he had somehow become tuned in to forces that nobody could understand. 'Best to forget it,' he advised. Janet said there were things that couldn't be explained. 'There just aren't answers,' she would say in her exasperated tone of voice.

The official explanation which was being given in the newspapers for the phenomena at Aragarr was that, a) the village had been hit by an earthquake, and b) the animals had behaved as they had because of some sixth sense had warned them of the earthquake. All the stories about Meg Rees and anything that smacked of the paranormal were ignored. McBaith had found it irritating at first but then had become resigned about it. Before his visit to Aragarr, how would he have reacted to stories about people seeing things from another time or a seer who had come back for revenge? He knew the answer to that one. He'd have laughed his head off.

'There's one thing ... about me I still can't figure,' he said after a moment's thought. 'I keep going over and over it in my mind.'

'What?'

'That feeling of destiny that I told you about, that sense ... of everything being planned, of being led by the nose ... for a purpose ... '

'We all felt odd things ... '

'Yeah, but like I've said before I still feel them and I felt them even before I got to Aragarr. Something ... inexplicable was happening there, something we'll never understand ... I can hang in there with the idea that people picked up vibrations ... of danger, for instance. But I felt things when I was a long way from Aragarr.'

'Maybe you were destined to meet me,' she said mischievously, then kissed him, long and passionately.

After they had made love, the thought stayed with him, lingering in the back of his mind. It was true that with her everything felt so right. It was as if he had suddenly discovered a large chunk had always been missing from his life and now he had found it. But that didn't really explain the sensation of destiny that he had had for so long.

He's here, Meggy, to fulfil his destiny. Those had been the seer's words when McBaith had seen the seer and the woman in the Roundhouse.

Destiny. *Damn destiny.*

He tried to thrust the nagging thoughts aside but only half succeeded.

They lay on the bed for a long time, tangled up, half asleep, then, at sunset, they got up, showered, dressed and headed for the village and the excellent restaurant they had found there. They ate, drank and danced the night away then strolled back to their villa and spent half an hour in the swimming-pool, floating on a large inflatable raft and watching the stars.

After they had dried each other, they made love again in the shadowy bedroom, their love-making slow, gentle, devoid of urgency. When it was over the world seemed perfect and McBaith fell immediately into a light sleep, holding Janet close to him.

The whispering voice awoke him.

'What ... ' he gasped and blinked his eyes open.
How long had he been asleep? He was covered with a blanket and ...
The single word came to him again, a distant whisper.
He strained to hear it.
Then it came the third and last time.
'Seven,' it said. Like a sigh.
He groped along the blanket, searching for Janet, but the bed was empty.
'Janet,' he shouted.
She appeared at the door instantly.
'Yes ... what's wrong?'
'Nothing ... I just wondered where you were.'
'Just having a glass of milk. Were you dreaming? Your voice sounded ... '
'Yeah, I was dreaming. Come back to bed.'
He didn't tell her about the word.
About *seven*.

Twenty

After breakfast the next day, when they were about to leave for a bus trip to see the ruins of the monastery of San Anastasio, Janet told McBaith she felt dizzy and drowsy.

'I imagine it's a touch of the sun,' she said, 'I was out in it a long time yesterday and with my fair skin that's never a good idea.'

'We'll spend the day inside,' he said immediately but she insisted he go on the monastery trip.

'You must go. I want you to see the place. If you stayed here with me I'd only feel I was depriving you of something, spoiling your day.'

'But ... '

'No arguments. I think I'll just spend the day in bed.'

So he had gone on the trip alone and all day he had felt as if he was not quite himself. It was as if something inside him had been switched to 'automatic' and he was being steered along a course, his life taken entirely out of his hands. He felt as if he was on some kind of smooth-running emotional escalator.

He tried to explain it away by telling himself the fact of the matter was that he was missing Janet. But it was more than that.

He tried not to use that word again.

Destiny.

But that was what it felt like.

Like someone ...

something?

... knew better than he did where he was heading. Like there was a door around the corner and when he opened it everything would be revealed. And what about the number that had been whispered to him in the night? What about *seven?*

He shook his head, refusing to be harassed by the thoughts. In time they would all go away, he told himself. They were just a hangover from Aragarr, nothing more.

It was a long drive to the monastery and he found himself talking to some Japanese tourists but he was only half aware of what he was saying. He was talking about himself but it was as if a record in his brain was producing the trivial words and he had no need to concern himself with them.

The ruins of the monastery – the broken chapel walls, the remains of the huge arches that had soared over shady cloisters, the time-shattered monks cells, the propped-up wall that was all that remained of 'San Anastasio's House' – reminded him of Aragarr when he and Janet had driven back to it after Meg had been killed.

It had been as if the village had been bombed. Great trenches and holes were everywhere and dozens of houses were reduced to rubble. Bodies were scattered along the High Street and amid the fallen buildings, some savaged to death by animals, the rest crushed by collapsing masonry.

Thinking about Aragarr made him run through all the events of the past month of his life.

Then, as he was boarding the bus to leave the monastery, an image of a man leapt into his mind – a man with a huge scar on his forehead.

The seer?

Yet this man did not have the dead, putrid face, the rotting nose of the man he had seen in the Roundhouse. This man was young and handsome and seemed to be grinning mirthlessly at McBaith.

And the face looked familiar.

Like him.

He didn't bother to try to analyse the image any further. He threw it aside irritatedly and began talking to the Japanese tourists again.

When they arrived back at the village, he was first off the

bus, hurrying up the street, heading for the villa. He didn't know why he wanted to get there so quickly ...
(knew there was urgency)
(knew a door was opening somewhere)
... but he found himself almost running up the hill.

Striding up the villa's gravel driveway, he was surprised to see all the curtains drawn.

He threw open the door, puffing.

'Janet.'

Nothing.

A dim L-shaped lounge, a dark bedroom glimpsed through a door which stood wide open.

'Janet.'

The villa was empty. There was no-one there.

Then he saw the flickering shadows on the wall.

Something in the lounge.

He wanted to go back to the village, to get away, but he forced himself to walk into the lounge.

As the entire room came into his view, he saw the two candles on the table and the book which lay between them.

He approached it slowly.

A very old book, wide open where a cloth bookmark hung over the page. He touched the book softly. The white pages were yellowed with age, the brown cover cracked and worn.

He lifted the cover of the book and read the faded black print on the front.

Man of the Devil, an account of the life of the Black Seer.

This was the book Swinton MacLean had mentioned, he was sure of it – the definitive work on the life of the Aragarr Seer.

But hadn't MacLean said there were no copies of the book left? Hadn't almost all of the original material been destroyed in a fire?

Obviously Janet had managed to find a copy for him. Maybe she was hoping it would help him sort out his problems.

That had to be it.

Kind of her. Very kind.

But how had she done it?

He let the book fall open at the bookmark again and lifted the cloth aside.

He read: 'On that day, the day before Kenneth McBaith was dragged from his cell and cast into the flames, an advocate from Edinburgh, Stewart Duncansby by name, was passing Aragarr and went to the Roundhouse and spoke to the seer, saying he was a Christian man with an interest in the old ways, and the Seer said unto him "Remember the magick seven. When seventy-seven-thousand-seven-hundred-and-seventy-seven days are gone then will I return and wreak my vengeance and wash my hands in the blood of Aragarr. I have pledged a covenant with this place".'

But there had been no mention of Stewart Duncansby in the book Swinton MacLean had had – the book by Sir Roland Marlow. And that book had said the seer's threats were uttered as he was dying in the flames.

Yet ...

Hadn't MacLean said most of Marlow's book was written from people's recollections of the earlier book. Yes. MacLean had said it was like a man living in the 1980s writing about Waterloo. Things got twisted.

He read on: 'The Seer said: "There are glens beyond the glens and doors beyond doors. When the glens are aligned and the doors swing open one after another in a straight line that will be the first sign of my coming and the signs of my coming will be number seven. My Meggy will return to Aragarr then my wife, the Woman of the Seer, will call me back by the magick and that will be the second sign. And my wife will begin to call in the powers of death and fire and destruction and the people will feel the force of the coming power that will be the third sign. The fourth sign shall be that one of my blood who left yet never left shall return to Aragarr and he shall be the seventh son of a seventh son".'

McBaith felt a shiver trembling across his shoulders, running down his spine like small, cold rodent's feet.

He wanted to stop reading, to rip the book up, to destroy it completely, but his eyes kept reading.

"The fifth sign will be when my woman shall call in the powers on the Day of Reckoning to bathe Aragarr in blood and it shall be awash with blood. The sixth sign will be when Meggy who was my sacrifice before will be again, dying before, she will die again, my offering to the one who is my master. The powers of the light may try to protect her but there is one who is stronger. The seventh and last sign ... "

McBaith jumped and his eyes leapt from the page as the front door opened. Janet stood half in sunlight half in darkness for a moment, watching him, her face impassive.

'Have you read the prophecies?' she said at last and her voice was solemn. Her words seemed to echo around the room.

'Most of them. I ... Where did you get ... '

'Finish reading,' she said and walked past him into the bedroom, closing the door.

'Janet,' he shouted but there was no answer.

He let his eyes drop back to the page.

"The seventh and last sign will be ... "

He didn't want to read this, *didn't want to know*.

" ... will be when the seventh son of the seventh son ... "

Seven.

The word that had been whispered to him.

The magick seven.

" ... the seventh son of the seventh son who has carried out the sacrifice will come into my woman, the Woman of the Seer ... "

What could it ...

" ... and from her body will I be born again. Remember the magick seven."

The bedroom door opened slowly and he raised his eyes and watched Janet as she walked slowly towards him. She was naked except for a golden band which encircled her head, holding back her hair. From this band hung a dozen circular blue stones engraved with white half-moons back to back.

His mind swam but he managed to say: 'Where did you get this?'

'Did you understand?'

'Understand what?'

'The prophecies.'

'I don't ... '

She stopped in front of him and turned the pages of the book to a plate of a sketch. He looked down at it.

'Meg Rees,' he said.

She turned the page. A man looked up at him, a handsome, black-haired man with a large ugly scar on his forehead. The caption read 'The Black Seer of Aragarr'. No hanging, putrid flesh, no decaying nose. That had been the face of a dead man. This was a likeness of the man as he had been in life.

'The seer?' he said, looking at her.

She nodded and turned another page.

'The woman of the seer,' she said, taking his arm, her eyes holding his.

He wrenched his eyes away and looked at the third plate.

The woman was beautiful with long black silken hair. She wore a golden headband from which blue stones hung with white half-moons back to back.

He didn't want to see Janet there on the page, wanted desperately to pretend there was only a slight resemblance.

But it was Janet.

He slumped into a chair, his hands gripping her waist.

'I don't ... '

'There are glens beyond glens, doors beyond doors,' she said softly, 'moons undreamed of, worlds within tiny particles, shadows beyond the light.'

'Don't ... '

He felt so drowsy.

'I carry your child in my belly,' she said. 'I carry the seer to be born again. I carry Kenneth McBaith.'

'But ... '

She lowered herself onto his knee and her mouth opened over his.

'Don't speak,' she said, 'there is nothing to be said.'

He closed his eyes, aroused by the movement of her mouth, and was aware for an instant of a terrible stench, a death smell. The thighs and belly and back he caressed seemed for a moment to be cold and rotten and seamed. Like a corpse's skin.

Then his mind was flooded with light – brilliant, warm light.

'Shadows beyond the light.' She had said that. What ...

Then the light fragmented into a million particles.

Like diamonds.